I0726841

Aliens
AND THE
Dearly Departed

MJ MILLER

Aliens and the Dearly Departed,: Book Two A Luckland Mystery Copyright ©
2022 MJ Miller

All rights reserved. No part of this publication may be reproduced, stored in a
retrieval system, or transmitted, in any form or by any means without the
prior written permission of the author, nor be otherwise circulated in any
form of binding or cover other than that in which it is published and without
a similar condition being imposed on the subsequent purchaser.

This is a work of fiction. Names, characters, places, and incidents are either
the product of the author's imagination or are used fictitiously, and any
resemblance to actual persons living or dead, business establishments,
events, or locales, is entirely coincidental.

ISBN 978-1-953100-51-1

Cover design by dreams2media

Editor: Penny Brandon

First Trade Paperback Printing by Scarsdale Publishing December 2022

10 9 8 7 6 5 4 3 2

If you purchased this book without a cover, you should be aware that this
book is stolen property. It was reposted as "unsold and destroyed" to the
publisher, and neither the author nor the publisher has received any payment
for this "stripped book."

SP

For Eric, 7 down 93 to go.

This is for my brother who wrote over 100 books but died before my first book was published.

TRADEMARK ACKNOWLEDGEMENTS
BRAND AND CHARACTER NAMES USED:

- Sherlock - *Conan Doyle Estate Ltd owns trademark for the name Sherlock (Holmes)*
- Watson - *Conan Doyle Estate Ltd owns trademark for the name Watson*
- Jon Bon Jovi - *trademark owned by Bon Jovi Productions, Inc*
- Inspector Clouseau - *rights owned by Metro-Goldwyn-Mayer*
- Google - *registered trademark owned by Google LLC, under parent company Alphabet, Inc*
- Kemosabe - *rights owned by NBC Universal*
- Indiana Jones - *trademark owned by Lucasfilm Ltd LLC*
- Magnum PI - *registered trademark for Universal City Studios LLC*
- Groucho - *registered trademark of Groucho Marx Productions*
- Harpo - *registered trademark of Groucho Marx Productions*
- Agent 99 *(Get Smart, CBS Media Ventures)*
- Marvel - *The Walt Disney Company owns Marvel Entertainment brand but doesn't own rights for all characters; Marvel Characters Inc has trademark for lots of products*
- Colonel Mustard *Copyrighted by Hasbro*
- Ghostbusters (movie) *Columbia Pictures*

- Crimson and Clover (song) *Tommy James & The Shondells*
- Captain Crunch *(cereal brand) The Quaker Oats Company*
- Pippi Longstocking *Astrid Lindgren*
- Dudley Do Right *JMM Lee Properties*
- It's My Life *Bon Jovi Productions, Inc*
- James Patterson *Author*
- Calvin Klein *(designer brand) the Trustee of the Calvin Klein Trademark Trust*
- Elton *(musician) Elton John name mention only*
- Village People *(band) name mention only*
- Gloria Gaynor, I Will Survive *(artist and song) Gloria Gaynor*
- Peter Pan *(character) J.M. Barrie*
- Saturday Night Fever *(movie) Paramount Pictures Corporation*
- Houdini *(magician) name mention only*
- Yoda *(character from Star Wars) Lucasfilm Ltd. LLC*
- Jedi *(same) Lucasfilm Ltd. LLC*
- Mr. Clean *(brand) Procter & Gamble Company*
- Grinch *(character) Dr. Seuss*
- Milky Way *(candy bar) Mars, Incorporated*
- Fester *(character) from The Addams Family, Metro-Goldwyn-Mayer*
- iPad
- Ouija
- Antiques Roadshow
- Encyclopedia Brown
- Globe Magazine
- Agent K: *Men in Black. Columbia Pictures, Amblin Entertainment, Parkes/MacDonald Productions*
- E.T. *Universal Pictures*

- NASA
- It's Raining Men *Weather Girls Columbia Records and CBS Records International. Written by Paul Jabara and Paul Shaffer*
- Will & Grace *NBC*
- Swiss Army Knife: *Victorinox*

CHAPTER ONE

BABS: COME TO PRU'S. EMERGENCY.

Babs was my twin sister, and she was serious. Or seriously itching for trouble. I sighed and got out of bed, then tripped over 99, my feline ball of white fur. With only one eye barely open, I looked for a pair of shorts and a t-shirt, preferably clean, and prayed there would be coffee waiting for me when I got downstairs. That was one of the fabulous things I'd begun to discover about having a significant other. While I battled with my tangled-up mane of red curls, Devon dressed and made me coffee. I didn't have to say a word—he just knew, for which I was extremely grateful.

Fifteen minutes later, I was out the door, heading over to Pru's, coffee, laptop, and camera in hand, with Devon by my side. I looked at him and marveled over what had brought us together. Having grown up with him as the literal boy next door, he'd been more of an annoyance than anything else. Then he'd left for college. When he'd recently returned to help us find some missing shoeboxes, he'd pretended to be a private detective, which naturally led me to see him in a different light. I smiled as I remembered how angry I'd been when I found out that instead of him being Magnum PI, he was FBI, which took some getting used to. Not as much as getting used to the fact his Aunt Matilda had turned out to be his mother. That was going to take a lot longer to digest.

On the short drive to Pru's house, I wondered what on earth might have happened to her. My first thought was that she'd fallen down the stairs. She liked to tip the bottle a bit, so her having a fall wasn't all that far-fetched. My second thought was basically no different than my first, though it had her falling off the scaffolding that surrounded her house.

"Do you think she's conscious? Maybe she broke a hip? Old people do that, you know."

"Easy, Red," Devon said.

Though my real name was Pippa, he called me Red, a left-over from childhood. There was a time, not long ago, I would have elbowed him for it, or worse. Not anymore.

"She's not that old, and I'm sure it's nothing like that, we would have heard the ambulance, and of course, I would have heard the call."

Point taken. As Luckland's new chief of police, Devon would have received some sort of notification that one of his citizens needed help, especially when said citizen was one of the four matriarchs of the town, who, coincidentally, were our mothers and their lifelong friends.

"Okay, Colonel Mustard, what's your theory?" I was still a little new to the whole investigation thing. When I thought Devon was a private investigator, I'd gotten the idea I might also like to be one. Even though Devon wasn't a PI, there was no reason why I couldn't learn from him, so I considered myself in training.

"My theory, Pippa, is that we have no idea what's happened, and so for now, we'll wait and see." He chuckled as he said it. He thought my jumping to conclusions was charming. Or so he said. I sighed. His answer was really no help at all. He was lucky he was more than hot, or I might not have let it go so easily.

We pulled up and parked in front of Pru's brick colonial, which would have blended right in if we were in, say, Virginia— in the woods somewhere...with a lot of fog. Her house had always been unusual for the Eastern Slope of the Rocky Mountains. Homes here tended to be built from wood and stone and were quite Victorian with their gables and wide inviting verandas.

Stepping through the open front door, we found the posse already gathered in the kitchen. The women had been friends since childhood. Inseparable. Matilda, Devon's former aunt and now his mom, wore a strange sari-like garment. She smelled like incense and wove her hands in the air while holding a bunch of twigs. Hope, who was the calm in the center of the storm, primly sat at the kitchen table, stiff as a board yet totally put together, as always. Over at the kitchen counter, Hope's fiancée Marcy arranged a tantalizing platter of breakfast treats. They owned a café, so the food was expected. My mom fluttered around the table, literally wringing her hands and pacing in different directions while muttering to herself. My sister Barbara, Babs—as we knew and loved her—stood by the door with her husband Tom, both looking as if they were ready to bolt at any second. The only person missing was Prudence Smalley herself. Definitely not a good sign.

Between my mom's muttering, Tillie's chanting, and Babs firing questions at Tom, it was chaotic.

"Ladies, Tom, if you'll all just give me your attention for a moment?" Devon asked, trying to instill calm and order. Nothing happened. He tried again. Again, nothing. I felt it was time for me to intervene. My dad taught me to whistle. Not the *whistle a happy tune* kind of whistle. The other kind. I put my pinky and index fingers in my mouth and let out a shrieking sound.

Success. The blissful sound of silence.

"Duly noted, Red. Thanks." Devon really appreciated my assistance in keeping the posse in check. "Now then, who wants to fill me in?" he asked.

Everyone began talking at once. I could have reminded him that the first rule when dealing with these ladies was to direct questions to one woman at a time. Addressing the group had been an open invitation to further chaos. I waited to see how he would manage this one. He looked at me, his eyes a silent plea, but I tended to lose focus with those baby blue greens flashing at me. I smiled and shrugged. To be effective as the new police chief, he'd have to master the essential skill of commanding the room.

Curious, I watched as he snatched up the tray of rolls and pastries from the kitchen counter, then headed to the table with it. It was a shrewd move because the cacophony suddenly died as everyone concentrated on picking their favorite.

"Well done," I said softly, so nobody else heard. I liked to give credit where it was due. Plus, it earned me a wink and a grin.

"Let's try this again," he said as he turned to my mom. "Kate? Can you tell me what's happening? Where is Prudence?"

"I'd be happy to, Devon." My mother always liked to be selected first. Though she hid it well, she had a competitive streak.

"I came by here this morning on my way to the store to pick up an old flask Pru wanted to sell." By store, she meant our family antique business, which she and my dad started years ago. "When I arrived, she wasn't here."

"What time was this?" Devon asked.

"Seven fifteen sharp."

"Perhaps she went to town? Maybe a brisk walk? Did you call her cell?"

"Don't you think we thought of all that?" My mom sounded offended.

Matilda jumped in at that point. "Oh no, Devon. When I was talking to Pru on the phone this morning, she said Kate was at the door. Then she hung up."

"What time was that, exactly?" Devon asked.

"Seven precisely," said Matilda.

"I see, and because Kate just said she came over at seven fifteen, it couldn't have been her at the door when Pru hung up," Devon said, stating the obvious, but then he asked a question that didn't have an easy explanation. "Mom, can I ask what you're waving around the room?"

"I saw this on a ghost-hunting show. It cleanses the home. Removes evil spirits," Matilda replied, very matter-of-factly, as if she'd done it before. I was pretty sure she hadn't.

"Aah," he said. "A smudge stick. Don't you need to burn it for it to work?"

"Only if you don't possess natural powers of your own, my dear." She said that as if it were an ordinary statement. "Don't forget, there is a special energy in Luckland. That's why Native Americans used to live on this land. The energy helped their special blend of elemental and earth magic. That energy also increases our abilities."

Devon and I exchanged a quick glance. I pursed my lips to keep from reacting. Devon did the same.

"How did you all get in here anyway?" he asked the others in the room, which I assumed was to change the subject. He should have learned earlier, but no. They all started talking at once.

"Door was open," said Matilda.

"Hope let me in," said Babs.

"Tillie let me in," said Hope.

"I came in through the back milk door," said my mom.

Devon turned to her. "Milk door?"

"Yes, of course, dear. Years ago, the milkman brought the milk in those lovely glass bottles and would come to pick up the empties. Houses like this have milk doors so the milkmen could come in and leave the milk in the mudroom." She could have just said the back door, but not simplifying anything was typical of my mom.

I leaned toward Devon and whispered, "You know they all have keys." I assumed he'd forgotten, considering he'd been away from Luckland and the ladies a long time.

Devon sighed. "Has anyone searched the house? Maybe she's here somewhere."

"But of course. How silly do you think we are," said Matilda. "I came running over as soon as Kate called. We searched the house together, then we called Hope, who texted Babs, who texted Pip."

There were a few things wrong with that. First of all, Matilda didn't run. Ever. As far as searching the house, I had my doubts. They probably just stood in the foyer and called out to Pru. I wasn't going to say anything, however. I wanted to see how Devon would handle it.

"Unfortunately, unless there are signs of foul play, I can't put in a missing person's report for twenty-four hours." He checked his watch. "It's only been forty-five minutes. I will, however, take a look around. I want everyone to stay put in this room, please. Don't touch anything. Just remain here. I'll be back in a few minutes."

I followed him into the hallway, but he stopped me from going farther. "Wait with the others."

"Excuse me, Encyclopedia Brown, but perhaps two heads are better than one?" I was referencing a book he used to carry in his back pocket when we were young. He was always pulling it out and reciting things.

"Might be so, Pip, but as your newly appointed police chief, I'm gonna have to go solo on this. Besides, I need you to keep an eye on everyone."

That last part was just to placate me, but I allowed it because I was, in fact, quite concerned about Pru's disappearance. Though that didn't change, it fell onto the back burner when the house shook after a thunderous boom from the basement.

CHAPTER TWO

It was so quiet I could hear a pin drop. We lay on the floor, Devon completely covering me. I didn't know how that happened except I remembered him literally grabbing me as if we were in a scene from an action thriller movie.

"Everyone okay? Pip?" Devon asked, his tone hushed.

"I will be, I'm sure. Right now, I'm feeling a little squashed," I said, assuming he'd get up. When he didn't move, I nudged him. "Hey, Andre, I could use a breather here." Devon was a lot larger than me—tall, broad, muscular with the kind of rock-hard abs I used to just read about.

He rolled off, none too gently, and had stood before I could even pull myself to a sitting position. I'd have to get him to teach me that.

"Stay. Don't move," he said as he headed back into the kitchen. I could hear them all in there, so I had to assume everyone was okay. No blood-curdling screams indicated dead bodies, so I didn't panic. Yet. I did wonder how long I was supposed to stay, however. Patience wasn't my forte, especially when I almost had my body blown into little, tiny bits. I wasn't exactly obedient, either. While I did take his request under advisement, there was no way I'd just sit there. I stood, gave myself a once over to ensure I still had all my limbs, then headed back into the kitchen.

"What part of don't move didn't you understand, Pip?" Devon shook his head in wonder, or perhaps annoyance, at my small act of rebellion. It wasn't the first time I'd not obeyed his *orders*. I was quite sure he knew it wouldn't be the last.

I didn't respond—too busy double-checking on everyone's well-being, which was a force of habit. As a photographer, I was accustomed to reading the room and getting a take on situations, and after a recent turn of events that had thrust me into the heart of mystery and mortal danger, I constantly tried to hone my investigative skills.

"Maybe we should look downstairs?" I asked, knowing full well the reaction I'd get.

"Maybe you should let me handle this." Devon gave me what I fondly referred to as the melting look. Meaning he directed his crystal blue-green eyes right into mine and tipped his head slightly. No woman could resist, and it melted me all the way down to my toes. I guessed we were at a stalemate. I really wanted to see what had happened. What if Pru were down there? What if she'd accidentally blown up the furnace? The possibilities were endless, and I took a few deep breaths to relax.

"Pippa, dear, let Devon do his job. Why don't you sit? Have a bagel," Hope said, no doubt trying to be the peacemaker.

"Yes, dear," said my mother. "Sit down and eat while Devon takes care of this."

"Try the rhubarb cream cheese. It's wonderful," Matilda said.

God, we were all recovering from a near-death experience

after an explosion in the basement, and they wanted me to sit and eat. I'd have thought any normal person would suggest we get out of the house and run like hell.

"Everyone, please, if you'll indulge me for a moment, I need you all to carefully, very carefully and quickly, make your way outside. Now. We could have a gas leak."

I knew Devon would be the voice of reason. I smiled, but of course, the rest of them all started talking at once, leaving me to settle it with another whistle.

"Okay, everyone, out. Now. Unless you have a death wish." That seemed to work. If nothing else, Devon needed to keep me as his sidekick to ensure cooperation in situations like that. The kitchen emptied pretty speedily, everyone filing out the front door and down to the street. Devon must have used his new handy dandy radio to call the sheriff's office as I could already hear sirens. Clearly, we had an emergency requiring additional assistance.

"You too, Pip. Get yourself across the street with the others, then get as far away as possible."

"And leave you here? Oh, no can do, Kemosabe," I said. I meant it too. Our romance was too new for me to see him blown to bits. If he were in danger, I'd be right there with him.

"There's a pizza with extra sausage in it if you do," he told me. "You also get to pick the movie Friday night."

"Anything I want?"

"Anything you want. Now go."

Devon appeared to be a fast learner. My weaknesses were food and sappy movies that ended with me ugly crying. So, I headed over to the group huddled at the end of the driveway, then rounded them up to cross the street. Not that I thought that offered any real protection, but if it made Devon feel better, I could give in once in a while.

The first fire truck pulled up, accompanied by several sheriff's vehicles and the gas company's truck. Martin O'Hara, one of the deputies, pulled up in front of us. He lowered his window and leaned across the console.

"Morning, ladies," he said, tipping his hat.

"Good morning, Martin. Have you come about the bomb?" my mom asked.

"I've come to see what's what, and until we know, I'm afraid you ladies will need to head back to town. We're going to need to evacuate the area," he said.

I braced for the reaction he was going to get. I was not disappointed.

"Oh, my no, Deputy. We can't go anywhere. We must find Prudence first," said Matilda.

"Yes, you see, she's the reason we're here, and what if she's trapped in there?" asked my mother.

"Officer Marty, I'm sure you realize we can all be of assistance if we stay here," said Hope using their familiar name for him.

"Ladies, please, you'll have to leave and quickly. This is a dangerous situation. There could be another explosion," he explained—patiently, I might add.

Hope shook her head. "Don't worry. We don't mind being blown to smithereens."

That pretty much summed up our little group. I waited to see how the deputy would respond. Trying to corral these incredibly stubborn women who had no qualms about standing their ground wasn't easy. My money was on charm, which was about all they responded to. He looked as if he'd been around the block a time or two, so I hoped he had a snappy comeback.

"Ladies, I appreciate your devotion to Miss Prudence. We all want to find her safe and sound, and if you truly want to help us do that, we need you to put your heads together and help us come up with some ideas. I think there's no better way to do that than over some of your delicious fresh Danish pastries at the café. What do you say? You can even ride in my car, and I'll turn the lights on for you."

Not quite snappy, but very effective. Thus, Babs and I walked back to the Blue Sky Café that Hope and Marcy owned while everyone else piled into the patrol car. I was pretty sure no seat belts were involved. We arrived before they did, which told me they somehow took a few detours along the way.

We pushed a couple of tables together so we could sit and discuss the current events, and we invited the deputy to stay and have a Danish with us. I had a feeling he would have stayed, either way, ready with some questions.

The deputy's approach was very different from Devon's. If Devon had been there, he'd have started firing off questions immediately. All business. Martin O'Hara just sat back and let them all talk. His approach was something I'd have to consider. If I were to become a first-rate investigator, I needed to learn various techniques. Maybe the fact Martin grew up alongside our informal women's club and graduated high school with them called for a distinctive style. Once we were all away from the scene of the crime, as it were, the ladies addressed him far less formally. He was simply Marty.

I eventually got a little impatient. I needed some updates.

"Do you know anything more? Can you find out what they know?" I asked him point blank. "Maybe you can ask Devon for an update." I could have asked Devon myself, of course, but I assumed he was busy investigating.

"These things take time, Pippa," he said.

"What if Pru doesn't have any time?" No sooner had I asked than I realized I'd probably stepped over some invisible line. Fear turned his face a few shades paler. From his reaction, I would have said he had a thing for Pru. Perhaps his concern was more than professional. With my curiosity peaked, I would have loved to know more. However, there was no time to ponder Prudence and Martin's relationship as we really, really needed to find her.

CHAPTER THREE

Several hours later, the sheriff gave the ladies the all-clear to return home. Evidently, there was no gas leak at Pru's. The ATF investigator had done whatever they did and gathered evidence, as had the fire chief. If they knew what had happened, they sure weren't telling us.

My mom, Matilda, Hope, and Marcy decided it was best if they went to my mom's house to figure out where Pru had gone. The four best friends all lived on the same street, literally next door to one another. From what I'd been told, each woman had inherited the house from their parents, who had inherited it from their parents, going back to the first founding families— that was how far back our ancestry went.

Instead of going home, I headed to Ye Olde Antique Shoppe, our family store. My mom and dad bought it right after they were married. My dad was the sales guru, and my mom was the buyer. My dad was quite charming and could pretty much sell anything to anyone, anytime. Far from a snake oil salesman, he was so lovable the ladies, and the men for that matter, just couldn't seem to say no. He once sold Mrs. Jenkins, my old math teacher, an abacus that he told her he'd *heard* belonged to a Ming Dynasty Emperor. It remained in her classroom until she retired, ensuring her students learned the history of a Chinese Abacus in the one to five ratio. I wasn't saying what my dad told her wasn't true, though she might not want to show up at the Antiques Roadshow with it.

I strode through the backdoor, jingling the bells that had hung there forever, a type of early warning system. Luckland wasn't notorious for its crime rate, so typically, we only needed bells. I found my dad in the back workshop—a cleared-out space where he kept his woodworking gear and tools. He worked on what appeared to be a fascinating statue that looked remarkably like a sculptured silhouette of an alien. The statue also looked as if it could grace the cover of the National Globe, with a screaming headline "They're baaaaaack," and the subhead "Iowa woman makes breakfast for early morning visitor."

"Okay, I'll bite. Where'd you get that, and what is it?" I asked as I gave him a hug.

"Well, Pip. Prudence brought it in the other day. She was very secretive but asked me to tell her what I thought it might be. I didn't pay much attention to it at the time, but as soon as your mom said something seems to have happened to Pru, I thought I'd take a look."

"So, do you have any ideas?" I didn't see how any of this related to her disappearance. Not at all.

"Well, I have no idea what it's made of, which is interesting. It doesn't respond to any of the metal tests. Quite puzzling, really." My dad seemed frustrated, which was odd because he was very good at identifying materials and dating them.

"Maybe Devon can help," I said.

Devon was quite brilliant. He always had been. Back in high

school, he was the nerdy future professor type. At least, that was how I saw him. Just then, as if the mention of his name had conjured him, he slipped in through the shop's back door, setting off the little bells. My stomach flipped when I saw him. Our relationship was still in the honeymoon phase, and he was incredibly handsome—tall and lean with beautiful eyes, long dark lashes, and a mop of golden-brown hair that always looked a bit mussed. Legend had it he looked just like his biological father, who had an uncanny resemblance to Jon Bon Jovi. Watching Devon approach, I fleetingly wondered how I, Pippa O'Leary, freckle-faced, red-haired, and a tad awkward, landed such a specimen. Then I reminded my thirty-year-old self I was quite worthy. Some of us took a while to grow into ourselves. That was all. Devon certainly did. Or maybe it just took me a while to see him for who he was.

"Any word on Pru?" I asked him immediately.

"Not yet, but we're working on a few leads," he replied somewhat absently.

"What do you mean?"

"Nothing, nothing, just working on it. That's all. What do we have here?" He pointed to the alien sculpture lying on the table.

"We're not quite sure," said my dad. "I can't make out what it is at all. I've run test after test. Unidentifiable materials. Prudence brought it in. What do you make of it?"

"Let me see." Devon crouched next to the table and rubbed his hands over the smooth, gleaming figurine, peering here and there.

"Maybe it's a moon rock," I said. After all, if it wasn't from any sort of composite material here on Earth, then other possibilities existed. "In fact, maybe it was a meteorite found by an artist who lived out in the wilderness, and he used it to create this masterpiece!" I smiled, quite triumphant in my conclusion.

Both men looked at me with raised brows.

"Fine, if you have something better, then share it. Dad? Anything? Agent K? How about you?" I waited a heartbeat. "Yes, I thought as much."

"Looks like an elf, don't you think?" Devon asked my dad.

"A gnome, yes, I can see that."

At that point, I headed to the front of the store and made myself useful doing inventory. How they didn't see the resemblance to E.T., I simply didn't know. I certainly saw it, which reminded me of when my best friend Dani and I had dressed as Ghostbusters for Halloween. We were twelve. We'd rung the bell at Prudence's house, and when she answered, instead of giving us candy, she made us come inside and told us to go downstairs and exterminate the visitors. We didn't question her, but simply went into her basement, pretended to eliminate the vermin, collected our candy, and left. That statue was the item we'd "blasted." I wondered if Devon would deem that information important. With a sigh, I headed back to the workshop to offer up the additional revelation.

"Say, Devon, remember that Halloween when Dani and I dressed up as Ghostbusters and wouldn't let you go to Pru's to trick or treat?"

"Vaguely. You threatened to shoot your lasers at me," he replied, smirking. "Plus, you told me she was all out of Milky Ways."

"Well, Pru had us go down to the basement to destroy unwanted guests. There weren't any, but a figure in the corner looked just like this guy." I nodded toward the statue.

"Maybe we ought to gather up the troops and discuss this," Devon said. He meant the ad-hoc ladies' auxiliary, of course. My mom and her besties—the self-appointed matriarchs of Luckland.

Leaving my dad to investigate the alien being further, or

whatever it was, Devon and I drove to my mother's house. We used my Jeep since Devon was still awaiting the promised patrol car that came with his job. The mayor had told him the car was on order, though I was sure it wasn't the mayor who'd ordered it. It had to be the ladies' doing.

My parents lived in separate dwellings next door to each other. They weren't divorced but had difficulty sharing living space due to her clutter problem. Or so I assumed. Considering they still spent all their time together, their living arrangements were a little odd.

We found my mom, Matilda, Hope, and her fiancée Marcy, out back on the patio, around the umbrella table where they tended to hold their summits. Babs was MIA, as usual. My mom said something about Leah needing a pedicure. Leah was my three, going on thirty-year-old niece.

It was odd seeing the ladies without Prudence. They were usually attached at the hip most times. They'd been like that since they were little girls. Devon and I had recently stumbled upon a scrapbook of Matilda's, where we got a glimpse of their extraordinary lifelong friendship.

The women were eerily quiet. They should have been chatting away furiously, all talking over one another, so the silence was extremely unnerving. They all looked at us expectantly. Hopefully.

Devon shook his head and pulled out a chair for me. He was nothing if not well-mannered, which could be associated with his FBI training. He wasn't well-mannered as a boy.

I reached toward the center of the table and grabbed a few glasses, then poured Devon and me each a glass of iced tea, which I hoped would inject some normalcy into the situation. If we appeared calm, it might reduce the tension.

"Ladies, do any of you know anything about the statue Prudence asked Colin to look at?" he asked, his tone casual.

They all started speaking at once.

"One at a time, please," he said as he seemed to remember to question them individually and not as a whole. "Kate? How about you start."

CHAPTER FOUR

AN ACTRESS AT HEART, MY MOTHER COMMANDED THE ROOM. PETITE, with a blonde bob and almost fairy-like features, she stood as if she were the lead in a strange play and began her recitation.

"It began with her first husband," she stated emphatically. "She was the first of us to get married, you know, back in eighty-two." Then she paused as if what she'd said explained everything when it didn't explain a thing.

"Go on, tell us about him. I don't know much, except it was a short marriage. Is that right?" Devon looked at me for confirmation. I shrugged because I was equally in the dark about Pru's mysterious past.

"Well, he was no good. The filthy pig was very abusive," Mom said.

"What happened to him?" Devon asked.

"We don't know, and we don't care!" Matilda said, straightening her shoulders. "Pru called us one night from Denver where they were living, said she'd had enough and was coming home."

Hope jumped in at that point. "She arrived a few hours

later, looking the worse for wear, mind you, and we sat with her on the sofa and cried all night with her."

"By morning, she picked herself up and dusted herself off, and we never spoke of him again," my mom declared, a distinct bite to her tone.

"I'm sorry, Mom, how does it relate to the Martian at the store?" I really didn't see any connection, and by the confusion in Devon's eyes, he didn't either.

"Patience, Pip, just getting to that. When we unloaded Pru's car the next day, the statue was in the trunk. I asked her what it was, but she had no idea. She said she'd never seen it before. So, we just put it in her parent's basement, which became Pru's when her parents died."

"What was the ex-husband's name?" Devon asked.

"Wally. Wally Noble. And he was anything but!" replied Matilda.

Devon nodded, noting down the name. "When were they married, do you remember?"

"Of course we do. We were all there. Even though they'd eloped, you don't think we'd miss that do you?" My mom seemed offended by the question. "Just a moment, and I'll fetch a photo," she said. That got my attention. My mother hadn't shared photos of Pru's wedding with me before.

She returned with a small photo album—the souvenir kind. She opened it and flipped it around, laying it on the table so we all could see. The photo was not of the Pru I knew and loved, but a much different Pru. She wore a white gown that pouffed everywhere, just like her hair, which looked teased and blown. I thought her hair was also her original color, a rich auburn. Standing next to her, I assumed, was Wally. He was short and wiry and wore a tux, green no less, with a ruffled shirt. He had a handlebar mustache and was certainly not what I expected at all. I had envisioned some tall, dark, and handsome guy. The irresistible kind a young woman would run off and elope with.

"Mom, for an elopement, they sure are dressed up." I tried to say something noncommittal because I certainly didn't want to insult Prudence's taste in men.

"Well, back then, a lot of people eloped, I suppose. They had rental places to get the clothes. I'm sure they still do. Why buy something you'll only wear once!" Considering my mother was quite the hoarder and bought practically everything she saw, her statement made me grin.

"Oh yes, Pip, we all got something nice to wear," Hope said as she flipped to the next photo, which showed the girls in all their splendor. I supposed that was what bridesmaids wore in the early eighties. The dresses were crimson and puffy.

"Was it around Christmas?" I asked. Green tux and red dresses? I figured it must have been.

"Why no, dear," said Matilda. "Crimson and clover, you know?"

It was all I could do not to spit out the tea I'd been drinking.

"Oh, I loved that song!" said my mom. Then Matilda started singing. Known as the karaoke queen of Luckland, she had quite the voice. The next thing I knew, the three women began a rousing chorus with Matilda holding an invisible microphone. The look on Devon's face was priceless.

I laughed. "What, Dev? You'd forgotten?"

"Apparently, I had, but this is quite the reminder," he said with a grin. Prudence was missing, and there we were, acting a bit silly. Maybe it seemed disrespectful, but it certainly broke the tension.

"Ladies, can we focus here?" asked Devon a few choruses later.

Just as fast, they sobered right up, figuratively of course.

"Of course, Devon," my mother said. "Quite right. Now,

where were we? Oh yes, they were only married a few weeks. Nobody has seen Wally since, and the statue of unknown origin has remained in her basement. I've offered to sell it at the shop many times, but Pru insisted on keeping it. Until it seems, the other day. She just up and brought it in and asked Colin to check it out."

I frowned. "When you say nobody has seen Wally since, what do you mean? He just...vanished?"

"Exactly, and good riddance," Matilda said.

"Where did she meet Wally?" Devon asked. "Was he from Luckland?"

"Oh, no, he most certainly wasn't," said Hope. "She met him in college. He was from the town just north of Denver. You know the one." Hope always thought we knew what she wasn't saying. As an aspiring playwright, she should be good with words and descriptions. Apparently, that skill only appeared when writing.

"Pru wanted to be an astronaut," said Matilda. "She wasn't physically cut out for it, not tall enough, so she studied astrophysics. She hoped to discover the nearest Earth-like planet. She's the brains among us, you know."

I'd never heard any of that before. The Prudence I'd known had always been a little loopy. She had an affinity for the bottle and was always just a drink away from an intervention. Her brief but crazy marriage and her apparent genius IQ put a whole new spin on things for sure.

I started making mental notes. Devon stood and raised a hand to get their attention.

"I'm going to get to the bottom of it, I promise. In the meantime, just sit tight, and let's hope she returns shortly."

"You'll find her. We know you will." Matilda gave Devon a penetrating stare that seemed to scream, *don't you dare come back without her.*

As Devon and I headed back toward town, I began contemplating out loud. "I mean, think about it, Sherlock. Brilliant scientist marries abusive jerk, runs away, and now spends her days with her head in a bottle pondering an alien statue in her basement. There is so much more to all this than we thought. I think you need to file a report."

"I see where you're going with this, Watson." Devon shook his head. "Though don't you think you're letting your imagination run wild? We have enough on our hands trying to determine what happened in the basement this morning and where Pru disappeared to."

That was when it hit me. Not a lightbulb moment but a lightning strike!

"Devon! The basement. The statue was always in the basement. Always. Until the other day. Maybe someone was trying to blow up the statue!" I truly believed I'd solved the mystery of the explosion. I really was developing quite the knack for the unfathomable.

He seemed to ponder my explanation for a moment. As we pulled into the rear of the shop, he nodded and turned toward me.

"Pip, do an image search. See if you can find any other gnomes that look like the statue."

"You mean aliens, right?" I raised an eyebrow.

"Okay, search for *alien* statues that look like that one." He smirked and shook his head.

"Want me to find another Elroy? Say no more. I'm on it."

"Elroy?" he asked, chuckling.

"Can't keep calling him *thing,* can we?"

So, while he went off to do whatever police chiefs did, I went inside the shop to take a few photos of the statue. Then, after I'd uploaded them onto Roadrunner, my new laptop I'd had to buy after someone stole my old one, I began the hunt.

CHAPTER FIVE

Five minutes was all it took, and bingo.

"The International UFO Artifact Society Catalog, 1981"

I could only imagine what that was. I clicked the link, and there on the screen, in the classifieds of the March twenty-first, 1981, edition of the Weekly World Globe, was a small ad with a photo of Elroy, offering it for sale. A hundred and twenty-five dollars was steep for alien memorabilia back then, though the ad claimed it to be a *realistic rendition.*

I didn't know what Devon and I could do with the information, but I certainly knew it was important. I printed it out on the store's printer, then headed to police headquarters to share my find with Devon.

I took a slight detour to the bookstore on the way over. Something inexplicable pulled me there, and I stopped dead in my tracks when I noticed the hardcover book in the window, its shiny jacket featuring a photograph of none other than Elroy. The book's title read, *"Return to Roswell by Winston McConnell II."* I did not see how Devon could possibly have walked past it, but then I saw Ophelia Madden, the shop owner, carting a set of additional books toward the display to put out and realized perhaps she'd only just put the Elroy book there. I debated going in and buying the book or seeing Devon first. Book. Definitely the book first.

I hurried in to make my purchase, which Ophelia was quite excited about as it wasn't often a new display item moved that quickly. I was also excited, but differently. Though already shocked by the coincidence of the book, I couldn't get over the utter chance that my mother had recently purchased half the estate of one Nadia McConnell, daughter of Winston McConnell II. From previous research, I knew McConnell II was an adventurer and artifact hunter, but I didn't realize he had authored a book on aliens. Or rather, alien mishaps and crash landings. This was really quite extraordinary.

I ran across the street and down the sidewalk to Luckland's police headquarters, situated in the sheriff's satellite office. As I scooted between the desks crammed into the small space, I found Devon at his designated tiny desk in a back corner. I was sure the posse, once fully reunited, would take care of giving Devon a much more comfortable workspace. After all, they were the ones who created the position of police chief just for Devon. He didn't know that, and I didn't know how he could believe it was all happenstance. At the very moment he wanted to quit the FBI, a job appeared like magic for him in Luckland. He really should have figured out the ladies were involved.

I slammed the bag with the book on his desk.

"What's this?" he asked.

"Go on, open it and see!" I was very excited.

Devon was always exceptionally cautious, so he carefully reached into the bag and pulled out the book. The look on his face was priceless—a cross between stunned and ecstatic, almost a boyish wonder.

"Where did you get this?"

"I was on my way here when I saw it in the bookstore

window. Ophelia said my mom had handed her a carton of books, and that was in it."

"Why wouldn't your mom have recognized the statue on the cover and kept it aside?" Devon asked, looking a little confused.

"Well, she hates to inventory, so she probably just opened a box of books and immediately thought to send it off to the bookstore. I'm sure she didn't know the book was in there, but the fact is, Winston McConnell II wrote the book!"

"Why is he significant?" Devon asked as if he had no clue to what I referred. That was when I realized I still needed to show him the ad. Also, he would have no idea my mom had bought half of Nadia McConnell's estate. I reached into my other pocket for the folded-up paper.

After handing it to him, I quickly grabbed a nearby chair and scooted it up to the side of his tiny desk. I wasn't all that tall, but Devon was, and the two of us in his cramped quarters felt as if we were playing dollhouse detective.

"Seems to me what we have here is a very shady situation, Devon," I said with a combination of concern and intrigue as he scanned the printout.

"This, Pip, is amazing. A UFO society placed an ad to sell the statue? I wonder who bought it. How did it end up in the trunk of Pru's car? We need to investigate further."

The adrenaline rush I got from a really good photoshoot was nothing compared to this. "We do, but first things first. Come with me, Chief Marks, and prepare to be amazed." I stood and held out my hand, indicating he should come along—as a dutiful significant other should. He grinned and raised his eyebrows, the implications just a bit wicked.

"Oh no, dear boy, not happening right now. A different kind of amazement. Trust me. You'll love it."

The moment we entered the antique shop, we made a

beeline straight to the section of the store where my mom had displayed Nadia McConnell's stuff. The items had basically flown off the shelves, mostly from online purchases from our website, so only a few pieces were left. A small trinket box, a silver bar set, and a few knickknacks. The most interesting item was a sphere with orbiting rings around it, which looked almost like onyx but wasn't. It was smooth and black and shiny. Not a blemish on it.

I pointed to the remaining items on the shelf and table. "This is what's left of the items we received from Nadia McConnell's estate. I have photos of the others that sold though." I picked up the sphere and held it out to Devon. "Look at this. It's amazing. Dad says it's not onyx. What do you think?"

"I think your dad knows his stones," Devon replied.

Despite Devon's lackluster attitude, I smiled. "I did quite a lot of research, I'll have you know, and I learned some interesting factoids about Ms. Nadia. For example, her obituary didn't say who her mother was. However, it *did* say her father was Winston McConnell II, and her grandfather was *the* Winston McConnell, explorer extraordinaire."

"Hmm," Devon remarked. "I wonder what the connection is to the garden gnome."

"Well, first and foremost, it is not a garden gnome. In my esteemed opinion, it is an extraterrestrial gnome." He was truly barking up the wrong path if he thought the statue was of the common garden variety.

"Fine." Devon smirked. "Elroy E.T. Gnome."

CHAPTER SIX

AN EAR-PIERCING CRASH FROM THE REAR OF THE STORE SHATTERED THE moment and ended any debate about Elroy's origins. The only thoughts running through my head as we ran to the back were of my dad. Was he hurt? Was someone attacking him? Considering the Luckland Ladies, Babs, and I had recently recovered from being held at gunpoint by a notorious pair of thieves, it wasn't all that farfetched.

Seeing my dad without a mugger in sight, I breathed a sigh of relief, but I gasped at the sight of Elroy, splintered in a hundred or so pieces at his feet.

"Are you okay?" I asked my dad, though I fixed my gaze on what remained of Elroy. There wasn't much, except a strange, bubble-type container, about six inches long and maybe an inch around. I wondered how it hadn't broken like the rest of the statue. The container seemed to consist of dark-colored glass, so I couldn't tell what was in there. I reached down to pick it up, but Devon put an arm in front of me to stop me from touching.

"Not so fast, Red. You'll leave fingerprints." With that, he reached into a pocket and pulled out a pair of evidence gloves and a baggie. Always prepared. Always the boy scout, which was actually a good thing. As an adult, I could appreciate it. I hadn't as a child because, quite frankly, he was a disgrace to the boy scout uniform back then, constantly tormenting me with his pranks and teasing but being the golden boy for everyone else. My, how things had changed.

He sealed up the vial, or whatever it was, in the bag, then tucked it in his pocket. "Pip, go ahead and sweep and bag him."

"Come again, Captain Crunch?" I didn't mean to snap, but Devon really needed to refine his technique with me.

"Sorry, Pip, could you please sweep up what remains of Elroy and bag it up?"

"I most certainly can do that," I replied with a polite nod.

I retrieved a broom and trash bag, then got to work. As I swept, Devon turned to my dad.

"What happened?"

"Well, that's the kicker," said my dad. "I just stepped out the back door to rinse off some tools I'd been using. I wasn't even in the room when the statue fell. What I don't understand is how it landed quite a distance from the workbench."

"I don't get it, Dad. You weren't moving it? You didn't drop it?"

"No, I wasn't standing here at all."

Devon frowned. "Has anyone else been in the shop?"

"No, just the three of us," Dad replied. "If I didn't know better, I would have said one of the town's ghosts came in here just to cause some damage."

I sighed. Parts of Luckland were known to be haunted by those buried on sacred Native American ground beneath our town. The way the ladies told it, the ritual they did on Founders' Day was supposed to appease the spirits to stop them from rising. If the frequent mystical ghost sightings were anything to go by, the ritual wasn't working.

Devon glanced at me and grinned. He didn't believe in the ghost stories any more than I did. "Well, this is certainly unusual. Tell you what, I've got some contacts up in Denver who might be able to figure out what we've got. No time like the present to solve a mystery!"

I liked this side of Devon. When he left Luckland at eighteen, we were anything but friends. Now we'd reached adulthood, we seemed to have come to a new understanding about those volatile chemical reactions we experienced around each other.

He grabbed the bag with the shattered remains of Elroy then we headed back over to the sheriff's office, where I impatiently waited as he processed everything and called his friends in Denver for a pickup. I was eager to know what the stuff was, why it had been in Prudence's basement, and what was in the vial.

Once we were done, we headed back home. Well, my home, where he currently bunked. He didn't stay every night. Sometimes he stayed at Matilda's while figuring out his new relationship with her as "mom" rather than "aunt." Ultimately, though, the plan was for Devon and me to move into our own place together. The wonderful Luckland Ladies, in celebration of our coupledom, bought us a house. Not just any house. My dream home, which just needed a little repair. Devon and I called it Mystic Manor, and someday we knew it would be very special.

We entered my little rental craftsman through the back door, which led directly into the kitchen-cum-family room. I went in first and probably stopped a little too suddenly at the sight before me. The family room looked like a Halloween prank gone awry. Toilet paper lay everywhere, over the bookshelves, across the table, and over the recliner. In the middle, amidst a large pile of unrolled paper, sat 99, her little paws sticking out from her white fluff, hanging on to the cardboard roll as if it were treasure. I turned slightly to check Devon's reaction. Devon adored 99. He'd chosen her for me—the first sign he might have taken an interest in me, but I had no idea how he'd react to a misbehaving feline. Or female, for that matter.

He'd tightly pursed his lips, but humor filled his eyes, and his shoulders shook, an indication that if I gave him permission, he'd end up rolling on the floor, laughing and tossing the damn paper around.

"Go on, I know you want to join her," I said with a grin. I kind of wanted to see him let loose. He played with 99 and the toilet paper like a seven-year-old. Lightly tapping 99's paws when they got close to the prized roll of paper, then pushing it farther away. Boys would be boys, I supposed, but his playfulness spoke volumes about who he really was. Unable to help it, I got down on the floor with Devon and my feline friend and tossed a little TP myself.

It was kind of fun, I admit. Eventually, my stomach reminded me we hadn't eaten, and I got up to head into the kitchen.

"Tell you what, TP Man, you clean this up, and I'll scrounge up food," I said, then shook my head as I realized how foolish that was. "Never mind, I'll clean this up, and you scrounge up the food. At least we'll have something decent that way."

Devon was very handy in the kitchen. Me, not so much.

The day had been extremely long, with Prudence's disappearance, the explosion, and the annihilation of the alien statue —and it was only Monday. If things continued the same way, it could turn out to be a very long week.

CHAPTER SEVEN

After dinner, we grabbed some wine, a blanket, and my camera, then headed out back to wind down. A gentle breeze blew, and the clouds moved on, leaving a stunningly starry night to enjoy.

My new camera wasn't equipped for night sky photos, but I thought I'd play with it and see what I could do. The lens I wanted was out of stock, so I had to be patient. I set up my tripod and began fiddling with it when Devon suddenly went back into the house. I figured maybe he'd forgotten his phone or something.

When he returned, he sat down on the cushioned wicker glider for two he'd bought for us and placed a box next to him.

"Come sit, Pip." He patted the cushion. At first, I eyed him suspiciously, having flashbacks to when we were nine, and he gave me a birthday present—a box much like the one beside him. I went over and sat on the other side of the box, though I didn't touch it. Instead, I studied his face for clues. He had a very ornery expression as if trying to hide something.

"For me?" I asked.

"Clearly. Go on, open it." He seemed a little *too* eager.

"Will whatever is in there bite me?" That box he gave me all those years ago had a mouse inside, and just the thought still gave me the creeps.

"No, it won't bite. I might, but it won't." Devon grinned. I bit back a smile. His wicked grin was something I found increasingly impossible to resist.

Taking a very deep breath, I opened the box then looked at him in surprise. Inside the box was the exact night sky lens I'd been pining for.

"Well, how'd I do?" he asked, his tone apprehensive, though he had to know it was the most awesome gift ever.

"Hmm, I'd say you have now perfected the art of gift-giving. I'm afraid everything from here on out will simply be ordinary." His last gift had been an antique locket, complete with pictures of each of us from our formative years. I wasn't sure which of these gifts was superior.

"Don't bet on it, Red. Now don't I get a thank you?"

I leaned over and thanked him properly while still marveling at how kissing Devon was unlike any other experience I'd ever had. He was a giver, not a taker. He had a way of allowing me to set the pace before he dove in and took control. I didn't really want to know where he learned how to melt toes, but I was grateful he had.

The night was perfect for taking some spectacular shots, so I played with my new toy, enjoying myself immensely. After I'd taken enough pictures to fill a photo album, I sat next to him again.

"What do you think happened to Pru?" I didn't want to ruin the mood, but I couldn't get her disappearance off my mind.

"Well, it's just a hunch, but I think she's at the cabin."

I'd thought of that, and it made perfect sense. The cabin was a communal residence belonging to the Luckland Ladies and their families. Devon, Dani, Babs, and I grew up spending our vacations and celebrations there. Located at the end of a private road at the top of a mountain, it really wasn't a cabin. It was a six-bedroom masterpiece. Prudence would likely head there if she felt she had to get away.

"But why didn't she answer her phone when everyone tried to contact her? Why didn't she at least let everyone know where she was?"

"I don't know, but she must have had her reasons. Either way, it wouldn't surprise me if the others were also there by now. We'll probably hear from them in the morning."

"When will we have answers on why the basement blew up? And what about Elroy? Will you hear back soon on what his story is?"

"Well, hard to say. It depends on what the answers are, I suppose."

"And I suppose that's a terrible answer, Chief Know Nothing." I smiled so he'd know I was kidding.

"It will take at least a day or two. How's that?"

I sighed. "That will do."

"Regarding Pru, I borrowed something from her house today. Want to see?"

"But of course, Captain Obvious. Do share!"

He went back inside, then came back with a photo album. I had a brief surge of nerves. We'd recently come upon one of Matilda's scrapbooks when she wasn't around, and it opened a whole can of worms. The scrapbook, filled with old newspaper clippings and photos, revealed everything from Devon's true parentage to the source of the ladies' never-ending funds. From Devon's eager expression, I had a feeling we were about to discover a *boatload* of worms.

He handed me the ancient photo album, then sat next to me as I carefully opened it.

"Can you turn on the porch light for me, Dev?" We'd turned them off so I could take my photos. He did as I asked using his phone app, which was now possible because after a vicious pair of criminals had broken into my home, Devon had installed some fancy hi-tech security.

We began looking through the album, which lay half on his lap and half on mine. First, there were pictures of Wally and Pru, similar to those in my mom's souvenir album. Then we got to a new set of wedding photos.

"Oh my god, Devon, that's not Wally!" These photos featured Pru in the same dress but with a different groom. This groom looked older, dressed in a tailored suit, not a tux. He had neatly trimmed hair and a beard, and he might have been dashing if not for the fact he wasn't smiling. Not even a little. He had a very dark aura.

"When were these taken?" he asked as he peered at the photo. "Look at this, eighty-four. He flipped back to the Wally wedding. "These are eighty-two."

"So, after Wally vanished, she must have remarried. Can she do that? I mean, it's not as if she could divorce him if he vanished, and I thought there was a seven-year wait until the authorities could declare someone missing as legally dead."

"There are circumstances where you can void a marriage when someone is missing, presumed dead, before the seven years. I assume she evoked that law," Devon said.

"Okay, so who did she marry? Take one of the photos out and see if there's writing on the back."

He carefully slid the photo from between the acetate and the backing. It was one of those sticky albums where eventually, the photos got stuck if they weren't removed every so often.

"That came out too easily, Dev. She must have removed it fairly recently."

"Good observation, Pip, as always." He looked at me with one of his sideways glances, and my heart raced.

"Well, what's it say?" I asked since he wasn't sharing.

"Not a thing." He slipped it back in, and we continued looking. There were more photos of Pru and her new groom. Then we found one with the couple standing next to a telescope of some sort.

"Oh, pull that out. It's a souvenir photo. I'm sure it will have something on the back." Devon removed it, this time with difficulty.

"It says *Jon and me. June 1983, Chamberlin.*"

"Oh, the observatory! I've been there. It's wonderful."

"I'm sure it is. So, what have we learned?"

"That maybe they went to the observatory in June eighty-three?" Seemed pretty clear to me.

"That his name was Jon, Pippa. We have a name. We also know they met at the very latest in eighty-three." I thought Devon was somewhat glib about it. He had a bit of a competitive streak, like my mom.

"Well, points for you, Devon. I overlooked that. I'm still learning."

We continued looking at the photos, and another wedding set appeared. Things were getting surreal.

"Who might we have here?"

Pru still wore the same dress. Good lord. She seemed to like the dress better than the grooms. In the new photo, the groom was a big burly guy dressed in Bermuda shorts and a Hawaiian shirt. For a wedding. Huh. He didn't have the intellectual look of the last one. Nor the meek look of Wally. He looked simply like a guy out for a good time.

Devon took the photo out and checked the back. "October thirty-first, 1986. Halloween. Maybe that explains the outfit."

"Prudence sure likes to get hitched." I wasn't sure if I was the hitching kind. Or at least I never had been. I was still acclimating to a long-term relationship with a local man. My two cardinal absolute dating no-no's turned upside down by Devon.

"Looks that way." Devon looked at me. "But sometimes a marriage works, Pip. Keep that in mind."

Having parents who adored each other but couldn't live together made me question relationships. However, I truly hoped Devon was right and we would last the distance. Waking up next to Devon every morning had become one of the highlights of my life, second only to going to bed with him every night.

We flipped to the next page—and swore at the same time. Tucked between the pages was a printout of an article about someone named Jonathan Steppenhoffer, standing next to, of all things, Elroy.

CHAPTER EIGHT

We stared at each other in shock. Devon recovered first and started to read.

"*Professor Jonathan Steppenhoffer is shown here with a UFO artifact he recently acquired from Roswell, New Mexico.* Huh. Pip, did you bookmark that site you found with the UFO catalog from Roswell?"

"Of course." We ran inside, and I grabbed my laptop, quickly opening the site I'd discovered earlier in the day

"What was the date of the ad?" he asked.

"March twenty-first."

"This article is dated March thirty-first of the same year, and it states he just received the artifact. So, the professor answered the ad and bought the statue. According to the ladies, after Wally went missing, that statue ended up in her trunk. Jonathan then married Pru a few years later. Could he have put the statue in her trunk? Did he know Pru while she was married to Wally?"

"I think that's something we'll have to ask her," I said.

"Right, let's go."

"Where are we going?"

"The cabin. Come on." He was quite impatient. I thought that was my job—to be the impatient one.

"It's a bit late, don't you think?" It was already past eleven, and it would be a good forty-five-minute drive up there.

"I have another hunch that if they *are* there, they're up and ready to talk." Something was very odd about Devon. All those hunches and things. I knew he had them. Much as I always had, but until recently, he'd been very resistant to openly admitting it.

During the day, the drive up the mountain was extraordinarily beautiful. After dusk, however, it was gloomy, twisty, and creepy. The moonlight created dark shadows among the aspen and towering pine trees—trees that perilously leaned toward the road, giving off the impression they were about to fall.

It was close to midnight as we approached the cabin, which made for a stunning welcome. Solar lamps lined the drive to ensure we didn't stray off into the wilderness, and it always took my breath when I pulled up in front of the magnificent structure. The entire home consisted of walls of windows in every direction, offering three hundred and sixty degrees of stunning views. The interior lights sent a warm golden glow out every window. It seemed Devon was correct in his hunch that the ladies were awake.

"I bet they're out back with a bottle of wine, or three," I remarked as we pulled in and parked.

Just a few months ago, I was on my way to having my photo blog submitted to the Nature's Future Project to earn a spot doing on-site photography for a climate change campaign. Fast forward, and I was sneaking up on my mom and her besties at their cabin retreat in the middle of the night with a smoking hot guy to find out why an alien had crash-landed in our antique shop. Life did throw a curve now and again, but usually, it was Dani who had all the adventures. Maybe it was my turn.

No sooner had we exited the Jeep than my mother opened the front door of the cabin and stepped out, hands on hips and shaking her head.

"Pip, Devon, why are you here? You'll just have to turn around and go right on back home. We'll be back in the morning." She turned around, went inside, shut the door, and left us out there.

"You know that's not happening, right?" Devon looked at me, hoping I'd agree.

"Of course not. We'll walk around back. You have a handy dandy flashlight, right?"

He tipped his head and smirked before he grabbed a flashlight from a bag he'd stashed in the Jeep weeks ago. Then we headed off to find out what the women were up to this time.

We stealthily crept around back and climbed the steps to the deck. At the top, we could see all five women, including Marcy, sitting around the long picnic table that occupied virtually a third of the deck. On one side, Hope, Marcy, and Matilda. On the other was Mom and the lady of the hour, Prudence. Various trays of half-eaten food and carafes of tea lay scattered about the table. Tea, which meant they were having some sort of sober and serious discussion. That alone was unusual. As they all simply stared at us, the quiet was unnerving.

"Can we sit?" Devon asked as he went over and gave Matilda a kiss on the cheek. *Suck up*. They all nodded, and Devon plunked down next to Prudence while I sat next to my mother. Devon and I waited for someone to speak. Anyone. It was so quiet I'd have settled for crickets chirping.

"Are you here to inform us that you've found the shoeboxes? You know we're running out of time," Matilda said.

Out of time?

"No, Mom. We're here because of Prudence."

Prudence sighed. "Then I suppose it's up to me to get this

ball rolling. I assume you want to know why I ran away, as it were," she said, looking at each of the women as if for their approval to continue. They all nodded.

"My doorbell rang this morning. Thinking it was Kate, I opened the door. Perhaps it was unwise. Perhaps I should have checked first, but I didn't. There was nobody there. Just an envelope. So, I picked it up, and..." She looked at me. "Pip, you'll understand my reaction, I think. I opened it and pulled out the note inside. There, scrawled in a red sharpie, it said *'We're back.'* Without a second thought, I ran upstairs, grabbed my overnight bag, which I always kept packed for just such an occasion, got in the car, and took off. Came straight up here."

She took a sip of her tea, then sighed as if that explained everything. I glanced at Devon, who looked at me because what Prudence said made no sense at all—except for the part where she was frightened and ran away. I had a similar instance not long ago with a threatening postcard, so I did know how frightening getting something like that felt.

Devon turned slightly toward Prudence. "Do you know what the note meant or who sent it to you?" he asked, his voice kind.

"Yes, Devon, yes I do," she replied.

He nodded. "Might you share that with me?"

"Of course. It was them. I've always known someday they'd reappear. In fact, I'd begun to feel their impending arrival. I even heard noises in the basement, which was why I brought that alien in for Colin to look at."

"Just to be clear, Pru, by alien, you mean the statue?"

"Yes. It's been sitting in the basement for years, but I couldn't abide having it there any longer."

"Well, I think you should know that the alien-statue had an accident in the shop," Devon said softly.

"Is it dead?" Pru whispered, her voice trembling.

"If shattered in a zillion pieces means dead, then yes." I gave her a reassuring smile. "But we salvaged a vial that seemed to have been inside, and Devon has sent it to a lab."

"Well, thank goodness. Finally, someone will back me up."

Prudence was utterly sober. I had to keep that in mind, but I still thought I must have missed something. "Back you up with what?" I asked her.

That was when the ladies suddenly found their voices again.

Matilda spoke first. "Oh my, that's right, we didn't have a chance to get that far with the story this morning. You see, Prudence believes she had a close encounter."

"That was what ended her marriage to Jonathan," said my mom.

"Jonathan? I thought Wally was her husband," Devon said.

Clever. We didn't want anyone to know we'd snooped, but I was still stuck on the close encounters remark. Pru had said she knew they'd reappear, and it seemed she meant aliens.

"Yes, yes, Devon. Jonathan was her second husband," Matilda said.

Hope nodded. "Real piece of work, that one."

I turned to look at Marcy, thinking perhaps she'd have something to say.

"I'm only here for support. I never met any of them. Before my time," she told me.

That made sense. I glanced at Prudence, who appeared ready to go on with her story.

"As I was saying, it is definitely them. The aliens. They're back. That's what the note meant. I had to escape quickly."

"Were you kidnapped?" Like most people, I'd read the stories of alien abductions and watched all those creepy pseudo-documentaries.

"Pippa, it was an encounter, not an alien abduction. And

it wasn't real. It was that twit-face Jonathan, trying to frighten her," said my mother. "The weasel made Prudence believe she saw aliens. And we've spent well over thirty years trying to convince her aliens didn't exist. We haven't succeeded."

Red streaks of anger colored Pru's cheeks. "I *know* what I saw, Kate, and someday you'll know it too."

"Prudence, why don't you tell us all you can about Jonathan and your visitors? Then we can go from there," Devon said, his tone now holding a note of authority.

I really could have used a good Cabernet about then, but with Prudence being sober for once, asking for one would be inappropriate. So, I poured myself some tea and looked to see if any of the comfy chairs were around. I wasn't a fan of picnic benches. When we weren't using the cabin, most of the patio furniture got stored in an outbuilding. Seemed that was where the comfy stuff was.

Prudence nodded. "Well, it didn't all start with Jonathan. It started with Wally." Her voice was soft as she spoke. I hadn't heard her speak so clearly in years. Maybe never.

"We met in school, you know. Junior year. Astronomy. He was brilliant and kind. Very kind." Prudence sighed and shook her head. "We dated for a year and did what couples do after a year. We got married. A few weeks later, it was over."

"Just like that, it was over?" I asked, confused. Not by that little piece of trivia. I was confused by her tone. Her demeanor. "Don't take this the wrong way, but you speak about your marriage as if it were just a passing thing. Not the end of a rela-tionship with someone important to you."

"I loved Wally, but perhaps not in a passionate, romantic way. He wasn't Romeo, but I wasn't looking for a great love. I wasn't looking for anyone, really." Her voice held a tinge of regret.

There was way more to her story, but I didn't push, knowing there was much more to come.

"Beginning the very next day, and with each day that went by, he acted more strangely. We began arguing about little things. Then he began throwing wild tantrums." Prudence put her hand to her neck as if remembering something. "He smacked me. Twisted my arm. Tripped me going up the stairs. I'd never seen that side of him. The last straw was a wild argument over the radio. I was listening to Madonna while folding laundry. He walked into the room, glared at me, and told me that Madonna was the devil. Then he calmly walked over to the desk, picked up the radio, and threw it out the open window. Then he went out the window after it. Never saw him again."

"Never?" Devon looked angered by her tale, and I didn't blame him. The idea someone would hurt Pru or any of the ladies was repugnant.

"Never. I waited for him to return, with a baseball bat by my side, mind you. I filed a missing person report a couple of days later. Nothing." She took another swig of tea, then looked at us all.

"Just a moment ago, you said Wally was kind. Very kind. He doesn't sound kind," I said, trying to get that bit sorted out in my head.

"The Wally that left wasn't the one I married," Prudence replied. "Now, it's a little chilly out here. How about we all go inside and relax and get warm."

It wasn't really chilly, but the chairs were way comfier inside.

We all got comfortable in the cabin's main living area, majestic with its twenty-foot cathedral ceiling and floor-to-ceiling stone fireplace. Devon and I grabbed the loveseat by the fireplace, Prudence took one of the recliners, and the others sat on the sectional sofa.

Prudence leaned her head back and closed her eyes for a moment. I wondered if she was simply going to take a nap or if we'd get to hear the rest of the story.

"Prudence, what about Jonathan?" I asked. He *was* why we were there, after all.

"Oh yes, I was getting to that. Jonathan was our astronomy professor."

CHAPTER NINE

Well, that pretty much stunned us. At least Devon and me. The ladies, of course, were unfazed.

Devon leaned forward in his seat. "So, to recap, you met Wally in astronomy class, a seemingly nice young man, or so you thought. You dated for a year, eloped, and he went off the deep end. Subsequently, you married the professor from the class you met Wally in."

I waited to see what she'd say because she didn't know Devon and I had seen the photo of the professor and Elroy. The same Elroy who ended up in the trunk of her vehicle the night she fled Wally. Even I could connect those dots. Either Wally or Jonathan had put Elroy in the trunk of Pru's car, and the statue had ended up in Pru's basement. Seemed obvious to me. Though Devon liked to remind me never to jump to conclusions, in this case, I thought it was safe to say Jonathan was up to no good, though what his endgame was, I had yet to uncover.

"Quite right, Devon. However, it was quite a while later when I started dating Jonathan. You see, I'd gone home, as you know, then the following semester, I'd received an offer from the graduate school to continue my studies to get my Master's, perhaps even my Ph.D. Needless to say, I was very excited to do so. That's when I started working with Jonathan on his research, and one thing led to another."

"How long before you married him, Pru?" I asked because, evidently, there was more to this relationship than she'd said so far.

"About six months, I suppose. Too soon, I know, and it turned out very, very badly. I was always a bit impulsive. My upbringing, I suppose," she said with a sigh.

"Wait, what do you mean by upbringing? Didn't you grow up in Luckland?" There was so much more to learn about Prudence. It may have been late at night, but my brain was in high gear.

"Oh, I certainly did, Pip, but my father was a jazz musician. Piano. That's where I got it from. Before I was born, he and my mom ran off to New Orleans so he could immerse himself in his craft. They came back to Luckland a few years later, me in tow. My dad ended up teaching music over at the elementary school, and my mom wrote sci-fi novels under a pen name."

I didn't see how any of that made for an impulsive upbringing, but it wasn't my story to analyze. At that point, Devon must have decided we were going off track.

"What happened with Jonathan? I assume it ended in divorce?" Devon asked.

"Yes. Anyway, I'm quite tired right now. How about we all just call it a night? We can talk more in the morning." With that, she simply walked out of the room.

Right after Prudence had made her grand exit, the other women got up and said good night as well, leaving Devon and me with no choice but to also head off to bed.

When morning came, Devon was first up, fixing breakfast and brewing coffee. The women straggled in one by one, dressed a bit haphazardly. I didn't think any of them packed a bag or had anything with them. Devon and I were alike in that regard because we always had an emergency bag. A just-in-case bag of clothing and toiletries for whatever circumstances presented themselves. I assumed the women were stuck with whatever hung in the closets. It was hard to keep a straight face when they looked as if they'd been clothes shopping at the Halloween store that opened once a year at the mall. Matilda, of course, wore a flowered muumuu. Prudence wore shortalls. My mother sported a crepe skirt and peasant blouse. Hope and Marcy had dressed in matching Mullet Madness t-shirts. I definitely needed to finish my coffee before any discussions took place. Or maybe it was the women who needed the coffee.

"Prudence," Devon said without allowing them to settle.

Will that boy ever learn? I subtly shook my head.

"What pen name did your mother use to write her books?" he asked.

What? Forget the cup of coffee. I wanted the pot.

"I'm sorry, Devon. What does that have to do with anything? She didn't want anyone to know, which is why she used a pen name."

If I wasn't interested in the answer, I would have applauded Pru for her response.

"Yes, I realize that, but she's been gone quite a few years now. Do you think it still matters?" Devon asked.

"I'm sorry, Devon, my boy. I'm afraid I simply can't tell you."

Prudence was typically quite loose-lipped, so to see her super secretive was new, and I wondered why she had suddenly clammed up. It was quite unexpected.

Devon tilted his head. "Can you at least tell us what you and Jonathan were researching?"

"Oh, of course. The sexual behavior of extraterrestrials," Prudence replied in a relatively staid manner.

Coffee sprayed across the kitchen counter. I'd been right in the middle of a good sip too. All the women turned and stared at me. I supposed Pru's declaration wasn't news to them. I looked at Devon, who hid a grin. It seemed he found my occasional unladylike quirks quite amusing. My mother didn't. She looked horrified.

"Really, Mom, I didn't hit anyone," I remarked for good measure.

"We'll have to work on your aim," Devon said.

I watched my mother, knowing she would not like that one bit, but then her expression changed—from aghast to something that looked as if she found what he'd said funny. I needed to remember that for later. Right at that moment, though, Prudence's research took precedence. I was just about to ask more about it when Devon stood.

"Well, ladies, I think that's all for now. Pip and I are going to head back to town. Things to do, you know. Prudence, you'll have to bunk with someone for the next few days until we fully process the scene. I imagine you're aware that something occurred in your basement?"

Well, I sure hoped she knew, otherwise we weren't headed anywhere. I wasn't even sure Devon and I *should* head anywhere because so many more questions needed answers, but I guessed Devon had his reasons for wanting to leave. I'd just have to wait to find out what they were.

"Yes, yes, Devon. Of course we informed Pru of the bomb in the basement," said Matilda.

"We haven't established what it was yet," Devon said.

Pru tutted. "Well, I *do* know what it was. Someone, or

some*thing*, tried to blow up my basement, and I'm not going back until you've finished your investigation and it's safe. Rest assured, I'll be quite fine staying with Matilda since we all know you're bunking with Pippa."

I sighed. Though neither of us could deny that little tidbit, I didn't really want everyone knowing, but nothing was sacred in Luckland—except perhaps Pru's mother's pen name.

"Well then, perhaps we'll all regroup later in the week. What do you say?" Devon still grinned like a simpleton. He sure seemed to be enjoying all this. I had to admit, I was too. Life had certainly become more interesting since Devon came back to town.

Devon and I headed out a short time later, and as soon as we were out of the driveway, he clued me in as to why he'd wanted to leave.

"Okay, Pip, here's the deal. We have to go home and grab the photo album and put it back after you take pictures of all the pictures."

"Right, because we have to put the photo album back at Pru's so she doesn't realize we've seen it, but we want to have copies for ourselves."

"Correct, Einstein."

I didn't need Devon's praise, but it was nice when he gave it. "Can we please talk about this research business? I'm a little off-kilter after that revelation."

"I think we need to do our own research first. We need more facts. As I've got to do a few things at the office, can you look up the studies Jonathan and Prudence conducted all those years ago? I have a very strong feeling that's where all this is heading."

I had a very strong feeling he was right. His very strong feelings were becoming uncanny.

CHAPTER TEN

As we headed down the mountain, I began to think that researching the research of the sexual escapades of aliens might be a hell of a lot of fun—with Devon, of course.

"Hang on, Pip!" Devon held me back as he slammed on the brakes.

We safely came to a stop without even a smidge of a skid. Devon's FBI driving skills at their finest. He looked at me, the worry on his face startling because he was worried about *me.*

"You're okay, right?" he asked in a voice that would melt a glacier as he reached over and brushed a stray lock of hair from my eyes. We were having a moment, which helped drive the Prudence demons away. It also took my breath away.

"I think so. What was it?" I assumed a bunny or a deer. No, not a deer. I'd have noticed that.

"Well, that's just it, Pip. It looked like a child on the road, but it simply vanished. Maybe it was a shadow from the trees. Maybe I didn't have enough coffee this morning. Sorry. I think perhaps all this talk of aliens is scrambling my brain."

Devon didn't often have scrambled brains, and he wasn't afraid of things that went bump in the night. I studied his face, which I'd come to adore, and realized whatever he saw *must* have been there. A tiny shiver raced down my spine. Would any of Luckland's wayward spirits be all the way up here? Not that I believed in them, of course, but sometimes things happened around town that couldn't be explained—like how Elroy fell off that bench.

"Perhaps we better get a move on, or we won't get back before they do," I said as I leaned over to kiss him on the cheek. I'd only meant it as a gesture to say all was well. He seized the moment to kiss me back in an entirely different manner.

Once the windows of the Jeep defogged, I grinned. "We really *do* need to get a move on."

Devon dropped me off at home, then headed over to his tiny office. It was already early summer, and I still had to get started on my newest photography project, which was the endangered life of plants in the Rockies in the age of climate change. Unfortunately, that required transportation to and from my favorite hiking trail. As that wasn't going to happen today, I went out to my backyard with 99, Roadrunner, and my camera and started on Pru's photo album, which Devon had not so cleverly hidden on the counter.

I began photographing every item, carefully removing them to check the back for information. I'd never seen a triple wedding photo album before, and I wondered what kind of man-magnet Pru must have been in her twenties to have married three times. I'd gone through my entire twenties enjoying men, certainly, but never coming close to entanglements like marriage. I just wasn't the type. I wasn't sure why I had such an aversion to matrimony. Babs didn't, and we grew up in the same homes, plural. However, our parents seemed at times to be the poster children for a dysfunctional marriage, so perhaps my mindset had fixed on that aspect of their relationship.

While Prudence hadn't fared well in the marriage department, unless quantity mattered, Matilda had never married at all. However, she did have one incredible night with a Vegas lounge singer. That was how Devon was created—something he and I weren't aware of until recently. That secret was one of many the Luckland Ladies carried. Hope and Marcy were perfectly content, but marriage for them hadn't been an option until the twenty-first century. At least they could now finally get to tie the knot. Their wedding was sure to be spectacular, which made me wonder if any of Prudence's weddings were spectacular and if my parents' wedding was the bomb. Then, fleetingly, and perhaps for the very first time, I wondered what *my* wedding would be like.

Suddenly hot and uncomfortable, I continued photographing the photos of wedding number one. I stopped when I came across a photo of Wally and Pru in front of the chapel. I pulled it out, and lo and behold, another photo was behind it. Hidden. Wally and Pru, again, in front of the chapel, only this time with Jonathan on one side and the minister on the other. Jonathan? At their wedding? For an elopement, that was unusual. However, having a full complement of bridesmaids wasn't particularly normal either. What had Prudence left out of the story?

I had that odd feeling again. The fact she hid the photo made me decide right then and there that Prudence and I should have a girl's chat. I needed to know way more about this whole situation, and not from an investigative angle. I'd had my share of relationships, short though they may have been, and to understand what was going on with Pru and her many marriages required far more than surface information.

To me, she had always been this bundle of off-kilter energy. Never quite sober. Never quite calm and collected. I'd never considered what she may have been like back in the day, or what she was truly like as a person other than Aunt Pru. Perhaps a lot of people fell into that trap—not considering who a person really *was*, only who a person was to *us*. I needed to understand Prudence in a whole new light to solve this mystery.

I put the album aside, just for a bit, and started searching for the alien research of Jonathan Steppenhoffer and Prudence Smalley. The names were so unusual that the citations appeared virtually immediately.

Alien reproductive systems in the outer atmosphere.

Extraterrestrial life on Earth.

Human and extraterrestrial sexual interactions and reproductive theory.

There were about fifteen articles, but only those three had Prudence's name on them. The third seemed the most interesting, but I decided to wait for Devon to explore them further. What I wanted to know why Prudence believed in aliens. Maybe Jonathan thought of himself as an alien...

I considered myself as much a believer as the next person. I assumed aliens existed, of course. We surely weren't the only living beings in the universe, but believing they existed and believing they were on Earth were totally different concepts. Granted, there were whole government agencies devoted to aliens, and I wondered if Devon had any experience in that area. Maybe he was an MIB agent? Well, no, I already knew he used to be a cold case investigator with the FBI. Or did I? I'd have to be extra observant of his reactions to the stories I'd found, and though I speculated on what role Elroy played in Pru's and Jonathan's research, I didn't think I wanted to know the answer.

The thrum of the Jeep's engine alerted me to Devon's arrival, and I debated whether to shut down Roadrunner and head inside. However, I was too deep in the sexual habits of aliens, so I decided to press on—until I smelled pizza. Even top-notch investigators had to eat. Devon must have stopped at the café. Hope and Marcy had a fabulous new pizza oven, so if there was a bottle of wine and a nice salad involved, alien hook-ups would most definitely have to wait. My decision became a moot point when Devon came outside, bringing all the goodies with him. I put Roadrunner aside to make room for the pizza because it was hand food, making it messy and greasy and incompatible with laptops. The pizza even had my sausage on top, which Devon had promised me yesterday.

"I see you are a man of your word, Devon," I said just to let him know I appreciated it.

"You can thank me later, Red." He winked and offered up an adorable grin. "So, what have you found? I have some news of my own, but you first."

"Jonathan was at Pru's wedding to Wally, and their research was quite...interesting. I found fifteen articles to peruse. What do you have for me?" Too late, I realized my mistake. While being direct with Devon was very effective, sometimes he took things the wrong way.

"I have all kinds of things for you, Pip, but we should probably focus on the alien's sex life for now, not ours."

At his wicked chuckle, I shook my head, but inside I was laughing. "Okay, I can hold off. What did you learn today?"

"The International UFO Artifact Society, IUAS, which published the catalog featuring Elroy, was headed up by none other than, drum roll please, Winston McConnell II, the author of Return to Roswell."

"Wow, I did not see that coming. So, Winston was behind the kook's club?"

"Kook's club? Are you not a believer, Pip?" Devon seemed almost disappointed. "Then I wonder what you'll think of this next bit of news."

"I'm open-minded, really. To a point, of course."

At my statement, Devon smiled. "The IUAS is still an ongoing concern. They're headquartered in Roswell, New Mexico. Home of the first recorded verifiable alien crash landing in the US."

I didn't think there were many people in the US who weren't familiar with Roswell and Area 51. Even in Luckland, I couldn't go to the grocery store without seeing screaming tabloid headlines. Just the other day, "news" broke that a well-known reality show family was actually Saturnian spies.

"So, what do you say, Red?" Devon asked smoothly. "Up for a road trip?"

CHAPTER ELEVEN

"Did you take a wrong turn?" I asked as soon as I saw the road
sign.

"Very funny. Actually, Las Vegas, New Mexico is much older than Las Vegas, Nevada."

I did know, but it didn't hurt to let Devon offer his little trivia tidbits.

After Devon had phoned Belle Chantelle, the acting director of the alien worshipper society as I'd come to describe it, and she had offered for us to stop by and see her on Saturday, we'd rented a pretty snazzy eco-forward hybrid SUV because the Jeep wouldn't be all that comfortable for a long-haul road trip and left very early that morning so we could get to Roswell by mid-afternoon.

We weren't all that far from Roswell, but seeing a sign for Las Vegas, I couldn't resist the perfect place to stop for lunch. I had a feeling this particular Las Vegas would be quite different from sin city, the place Matilda conceived Devon, and I was right. Las Vegas, New Mexico, was just a larger version of Luckland with the same nineteenth-century frontier-style architecture. The historic downtown area was all spruced up with vertical street banners and colorful window boxes. We took a little drive through town before settling on a bakery-type diner with massive cookies in the window. Devon had a thing for cookies, which as far as vices go, I was willing to enable. We parked out front in one of the angled spots so common in small towns. My dad used to take me into Denver to practice parallel street parking because Luckland had the angled slots. He said it was because you could park more cars in front of a business that way. I thought it was because the older drivers had too many fender benders.

It took a little longer than expected to get service, but eventually, a nice young man came over and explained they were shorthanded as his wife just went into labor.

"Why aren't you with her?" I hadn't meant to sound snarky, but I was truly stunned the poor guy was working.

"Well, someone has to cook the food, and we always get a bit of a lunch crowd. Who'll feed them all? That's what Gina said. She said the women in her family can be in labor for eighteen hours, so I might as well keep the place open." He grinned as if it made perfect sense.

"So, if you get everyone fed, you can hightail it out of here, right?" I asked. Devon gave me a very odd look. I couldn't blame him. It sounded as if I was going to offer to lend a hand when he knew I had no culinary skills to speak of.

"That's about right," the owner said.

"Well then, Devon?" I raised my eyebrows and gave him as sweet a look as I could possibly muster. I was a sucker for a good story. Plus, I always believed in paying it forward.

I looked up at the father-to-be, whose name tag said Christopher. "Christopher, I suggest you enlist Devon here. He's very handy in the kitchen. You don't want to be late for your baby's arrival, do you?"

Devon was already out of his chair. "Lead the way." He

slapped our new friend on the shoulders. I sighed because that was precisely why I was hook, line, and sinker for the ex-FBI agent.

Within an hour, all the locals had eaten, as well as the few travelers, me included. Christopher headed off to wait expectantly for however long it would take to be a dad, and Devon and I headed back out on our adventure. He looked at me as he started the car—a very measured look.

"What? Am I wearing the sugar donut? Frosting in my hair?" Under his stare, I became the center of attention. Not my favorite place to be.

"You're really something, Red."

I honestly believed he meant that as a compliment. "As are you, Chief Marks."

I let him have his country twangy music the rest of the way. Not my thing, but all things considered, he'd earned it. Less than three hours later, we saw the first signs for Roswell. I wasn't sure what we were going to encounter, but I kept a very open mind.

The address Ms. Chantelle provided was a few blocks from the visitor's center, which was a bit of a disappointment when we drove past it. I expected a Star Trek style museum. Instead, the visitor's center for the most famous alien attraction on Earth was more of a cottage and sat next to a modern high-rise office building. We found the IUAS office above a flower shop. Another disappointment. As we parked around back, I turned to Devon.

"Maybe we should plan out what we'll say. Get our story straight."

"Just play along with me, Red. Follow my lead."

I'd never been on an investigative visit, so I wasn't sure what to expect, but I was for certain going to enjoy it. I hoped.

A woman, who I assumed was Belle, opened the door, and I

took a moment to stare. I'd anticipated someone eccentric. Maybe a Matilda sort, dressed in spiritual-type clothes. Or at least adorned with tattoos and maybe a large unique piece of stoneware around her neck. Instead, the woman wore a beige, tailored linen suit, her snow-white hair in a very elaborate French twist, a string of pearls around her neck, and a pricy-looking diamond on her right hand.

"Welcome, I'm Belle. You must be Chief Marks, and you are?" She looked at me pointedly.

"Pippa O'Leary," I replied in my most dignified voice, holding my hand out to politely shake hers. I had immediately transformed into the Pippa who made my mother so proud and me so uncomfortable.

Belle led us through a small waiting room, the walls crowded with strange prints of what I supposed were extraterrestrials alongside multi-media art pieces. I looked for something like Elroy, but Belle quickly showed us into her office, which struck me as very non-descript. It held a desk, chairs, and some certificates on the wall attesting her abilities in god knew what type of research.

"Have a seat, please," she said quite formally. I was really getting uncomfortable, but Devon had said to follow his lead, and he had yet to say a word, so when he sat, I sat, and waited.

"Thank you so much, Ms. Chantelle, for your time," Devon said.

Ugh. I so wanted to ask what she knew about Elroy, but I bit my tongue. Quite literally.

After some chitchat where I grew bored, she smiled. "Are either of you hungry? I can offer you a protein bar or some chips?"

I sat up a little straighter in my chair. I would have thought scones or petit fours were more her cup of tea. Junk food? How odd.

Devon smiled back. "No, thank you. We stopped in Las Vegas."

"Oh my, did you have a chance to visit the Mental Health Institute?" Her enthusiasm seemed a little...enthusiastic, and I could no longer keep quiet.

"Mental Health Institute?"

"Why yes. Originally, it was the New Mexico Insane Asylum. Quite popular among those who've had encounters." Her tone indicated it was a perfectly ordinary thing to say.

"Actually, we were planning on stopping there on our return, but anything you can tell us is appreciated," Devon said, implying we knew about this odd factoid. That, I supposed, was where I was to follow his lead.

"Well, as I'm sure you are aware, the asylum was built in the late eighteen hundreds, intended for those who were at the time deemed mentally ill in some way." Belle paused. "After the 1947 incident in Roswell, the number of patients skyrocketed."

She waved her hand toward the waiting room. "Those prints out there? All artwork created by patients, with the exception of the one on the back wall."

I hadn't noticed that one. Devon and I turned to get a good look.

"That masterpiece was done by our esteemed founder, Winston McConnell. The second," she said as if to clarify. I hoped she'd allow me to photograph the artwork, and I wondered if Devon would mind if I asked, but just as I glanced at him, he turned to Belle.

"Ms. Chantelle, do you mind if we took a few photos of the fabulous prints out there, especially considering who created them?" He smiled at her. The charming smile. No way she'd say no. I certainly wouldn't. Or couldn't.

"Of course, feel free, and please, call me Belle."

Permission granted. Progress. After a few more minutes of small talk, Devon and I went down to retrieve my camera bag.

"Devon, do you think there's something familiar about Belle?" I asked once safely outside. He looked at me, and I could immediately tell he felt the same thing.

"I think some people have a way about them that reminds us of someone else. Quite common," he said, though I didn't think he was all that sure. I wasn't all that sure either, but we needed to head back up and take our photos, then find out more about Elroy. That was our mission, after all.

I took the photos needed and spent a minute or five studying the artwork of Winston McConnell II. The pencil sketch appeared to be a swirling vortex with a vague alien-like image in the center, which I found fascinating. If I didn't know better, and I didn't, I would have thought he was on some sort of sixties acid trip. The artwork was signed and dated WMII 1968.

"Ms. Chantelle, Belle, sorry, can you tell us about the sculpture or artifact sold to Jonathan Steppenhoffer? The one we spoke about?"

"Of course. I found the ledger for you from eighty-one. The purchase was recorded there. Didn't have computers then. In fact, I don't use one now." She headed back into her office to retrieve the ledger for us.

Hmm. The IUAS had a website. So, if she didn't use computers, who kept the website up to date? She returned with the ledger and placed it on the coffee table. Then we sat down on the small sofa to take a look.

"Do you mind if I snap a photo of this page?" I'd have liked to photograph the whole thing, but that might have been a stretch.

"Of course. Help yourself."

I took a few shots of the page with the entry using a wide-angle lens, which allowed me to get all the entries on both sides. That was how I spotted another intriguing entry. I was bursting to show Devon, but I didn't want to draw attention to it in front of Belle, so I held my tongue.

"Have you plans for supper?" Belle asked, quite out of the blue.

I glanced at Devon. I didn't know if he wanted to continue our investigation with her or do something else.

"We do not, but we are open to any recommendations you might have," he replied in his formal agent voice.

"I know just the perfect spot. Why don't you join me?"

Really, we had no option but to accept.

Devon inclined his head. "That would be quite nice. We'd love to. If you tell me the name of the restaurant, I'll pop the address into our GPS."

"Oh, much easier for you to just follow me." Belle smiled, rose, and led us to the front door.

Once inside the car, I showed Devon the photo I'd snapped of the ledger. A few rows after the entry for the sale of Elroy, item AA1290, there was another entry for AA1294. Sold to Prudence J. Smalley. We looked at each other, fully understanding that whatever she bought, we needed to know what it was and where it ended up. It also begged the question, why didn't Pru mention it?

CHAPTER TWELVE

WE FOLLOWED BELLE OUT OF TOWN AND ALONG A RURAL ROAD, eventually coming to what appeared to be a ranch that had a horseshoe-shaped gate with a name carved across it. Belle Starr Ranch.

"She's taking us to her home," I said. I'd assumed she would lead us to a restaurant in town.

"Could be a good opportunity to ask her more questions," Devon replied.

I nodded, though I didn't feel comfortable with the situation. Belle was a strange woman.

We turned in behind her truck, then down a long winding dirt drive to just about the strangest building I'd ever seen. It was round with a smooth exterior of mud or concrete, like an igloo. I took a few pictures before getting out of the car.

The entrance curved like a porthole on a ship. Or a docking station on a spaceship. It was then I realized Belle's house was designed like a spaceship, and inside had pretty much the same spacey look. Devon glanced around as if what he saw was perfectly normal. How he did that, I had no idea.

She ushered us into what I figured was a great room or a multipurpose room.

"Please, have a seat," Belle said as she waved a hand toward what turned out to be a very uncomfortable sofa. "I'll fetch us something to eat."

As soon as she left, I looked at Devon and shook my head in wonder. He grinned, then put his finger to his lips, silently cautioning me to keep my thoughts to myself.

Belle returned, and we ended up dining in the great room while sitting on the sofa with a plate of assorted vending machine items. Cheese cracker sandwiches with peanut butter, apple chips, and my personal favorite, gummy worms.

Belle then provided unopened cans of soda. The sugary kind. Devon seemed to enjoy it all, so I pretended our "dinner" wasn't unusual, but only because I wanted to ask her more questions about Elroy.

"Belle, how did you meet Winston McConnell II?" I asked, hoping that would lead to finding more about the book he wrote, when he got Elroy, and from where.

"Oh, I started working for my father when I was just out of school."

Thankfully, though stunned, I did not spit out my food.

"You know, when the professor first contacted us about AA1290, we were thrilled to sell it. My father hadn't liked having it around, you see. He said it was creepy. Once we shipped it off, he became much more relaxed. At the time, I wasn't yet familiar with all the items he'd collected. Many of them were in his San Francisco home. I'd never been there."

So, Belle must be Nadia McConnell's half-sister. Same father, different mother. Though it was none of my business, I wanted to know if Belle knew about Nadia because, after my research, I was sure Nadia knew nothing about Belle. I was about to open my mouth to ask, but Devon gave me surreptitious glances that screamed, *don't say a word.* So, I didn't.

We learned a great deal more by letting her ramble on. By the time Devon and I left, we just needed to figure out how the information, if any, fit into Prudence's life.

As it was late, we headed to the hotel in town that Devon had booked for us.

"How crazy was that ranch?" Devon asked. "It looked elaborate, yet it wasn't a working ranch by any stretch. I didn't see any signs of livestock or anything growing. I do wonder what was in that barn. Maybe she's a doomsday survivalist."

"That would sure explain the vending machine snacks."

Devon grinned. "I noticed you didn't eat much, so how about we have dinner at the hotel."

"It has a restaurant?"

"Yep. I wasn't sure what would happen after visiting the IUAS office, so I made sure to book somewhere with a restaurant and a bar."

"You are a genius."

"I will remind you every so often you said that, Pip," he said with a laugh.

As soon as we checked in, Devon pointed to the attached restaurant. "I'll haul our stuff up to the room, and you go grab a table. Unless, of course, you want to come up there with me?" He raised his eyebrows in invitation. I seriously thought about it for a minute, then chose dinner. It wasn't an easy choice though.

When he joined me, we settled on burgers, which we practically inhaled.

"Okay, time for a recap," I said. "Jonathan Steppenhoffer purchased Elroy in eighty-one from Winston McConnell II, founder of a strange alien society in Roswell, New Mexico. A society now run by his daughter, Belle. Shortly after, Prudence

Smalley also makes a purchase from Winston, which, according to Belle, was an astronomical map."

"I'm not sure if that's relevant, but we can ask Pru," Devon said, looking thoughtful. "What is interesting and probably relevant is that the very next year, Steppenhoffer, who was Wally and Prudence's professor, attended their wedding. A marriage that lasted only a few weeks."

"Because Wally goes nuts and disappears," I said. "Then, Prudence heads back to Luckland with Elroy in the trunk of her car, which we now know belonged to Steppenhoffer." I frowned. "Remember Pru didn't seem to know where Elroy came from, even though there was a clipping of Jonathan with Elroy in her photo album? If she found out Jonathan had bought Elroy, why did she believe it was an alien?"

Devon shook his head. "I don't know. She never got to that part of the story. I guess that's something else we'll need to ask her."

"Okay, so a year later, she takes a position as a graduate assistant to the professor, and six months later, she marries him. Another six months later, it's over."

"But not forsaking love entirely, Prudence marries again two years after that," Devon said with a smile, which was kind of cute.

"Not to be Debbie Downer, that didn't last either. I wonder what happened to him?" I asked, mostly to myself. "Anyway, flash forward to present-day Luckland, when my mother purchases the estate of Nadia McConnell, the other daughter of Winston McConnell II. Shortly after, Prudence's basement blows up."

Devon nodded. "So, that leaves us with several mysteries. We need to know more about husband number three and the story behind Nadia and Belle. Then there's Elroy and the map."

Finished with dinner and our convoluted conversation

about alien statues and maps, we headed upstairs for some downtime. It had been quite a day, exhausting, really, with all the new discoveries and the long drive.

As we waited for the elevator, I turned to him and grinned. "Remember the last time we stayed in a hotel?"

"Last time? It was the only time," Devon replied, flashing a wink. "Someday, we'll laugh about our stay at the haunted brothel. I'm not sure I'm ready yet."

"Well, at least this time, you won't have to take the couch."

Even though we got a late start the next day, we decided to stop at the diner in Las Vegas on the way back to see if Gina had her baby. As soon as we arrived, I noticed balloons tied to each table broadcasting *It's A Girl* and *Isn't She Sweet.*

"How fabulous, Dev. They had a baby girl. We'll have to leave them a congratulatory note!"

"Oh, if you stick around, they'll be back anytime. Their apartment is just upstairs, and I'm sure they'll pop in here first," said a sweet, older woman who introduced herself as Anna, Gina's mom.

"She's coming home already? That's awfully fast," I said, surprised.

"Oh, they send the mothers home right away now. It's the twenty-four-hour rule. Babies are much better off at home," Anna said.

"Want to wait?" Devon asked.

As I needed the toilet anyway, I nodded. Once I got back, I saw Devon at a nearby table, making small talk with an older gentleman. Devon subtly waved me over, so I went and stood behind his chair, hands on his shoulders.

"Ah yes," the man said. "The old asylum. It's just a regular mental health clinic now, but oh, back in the day." The man raised his eyebrows and shook his head. "There were some wild things goings on there. You know they had their own little secret maternity ward. Some said the babies born there all had pointed ears and extra eyes if you know what I mean."

Before either of us could react to that shocking bit of trivia, Christopher and Gina arrived. The customers, mostly family and friends, cheered. It was wonderful to see and was the same type of welcome that would take place in Luckland. There was something to be said for a community. I'd always had that, though I don't think Devon or I had always appreciated it. He appeared relaxed and seemed to be enjoying himself, now chatting away with a local police officer who'd stopped in.

I began taking pictures, of course.

"Gina, I know you're exhausted, but how about you sit down, and I'll get a few shots of you and your little one," I said. "We'll get the new dad over here too."

"Oh, would you? That's awesome. Can you send them to us? I can get prints made of our professional homecoming photo shoot!" Gina beamed and pulled Chris down with her free arm while cradling her daughter.

"Her name's Francesca, after my nana," Gina said as she gently rocked the bundled-up infant, whose beautiful face peeked out from a soft pink blanket and tiny knit hat.

I took as many photos as I could of the new family, then with their extended family. I think everyone in town was suddenly related. I made sure to exchange information with Gina to email them a link to the photos.

Lunch was provided on the house, after which Devon and I took off back to Luckland.

Once we'd gotten on the interstate and Devon hit cruise control, he glanced at me. "I think there's something odd with Belle and her father. She never saw her father's San Francisco home, so it seems plausible she was born and raised in New Mexico, not California. Also, the fact she never mentioned Nadia had me wondering if she knew about her. Not that it really matters. Lots of men have children with different women, with none of them knowing half siblings existed."

"True, but I think we need to focus on that map Prudence bought. I think it's linked in some way, though I don't know how. We need to talk to Pru. Or I need to," I said. Not that I didn't want Devon involved, but I had a gut feeling Prudence's tale was something she needed to tell. Not just to satisfy our curiosity, but for Pru. She needed to do this. Of that, I was certain.

Ultimately, focusing on just what mystery we were solving was getting harder and harder. So many secrets. That was the thing about Luckland. It seemed to be a town fundamentally built on secrets and lies. I thought of myself as a relatively honest person, so the deceptions weighed me down.

Just as we pulled into the driveway at home, my phone rang.

"It's Belle," I said, checking the screen. We'd exchanged contact information before we left. I quickly answered. "Hello, Belle. How can I help you?"

"Oh, Pippa, I'm glad I caught you. I just realized something I think might be important." She sounded distressed. Or flustered. I put her on speakerphone, so Devon could also hear.

CHAPTER THIRTEEN

"I forgot to mention that the gentleman who purchased the statue, Professor Steppenhoffer, was a frequent visitor of ours," Belle said.

It was probably a good thing Devon had already parked because we immediately locked eyes.

"How frequent?" I asked, quickly holding up a finger, so Devon didn't reveal himself. She didn't need to know she was on speakerphone.

"Oh, he'd come down every few months or so. He and my father were quite good pals after a while. I did always wonder how the professor knew when to come, as he never came unless my father was in town. He was often away, you know."

We didn't know, but I allowed her to continue.

"I wanted to tell you because I didn't want you to find out from anyone else."

"Find out what?"

"Well, one night, after a bit too much at the local bar, my father informed the good professor about the Luckland gold mine and the map. You and Devon, of course, are aware of the legacy, but Jonathan isn't one of us. My father should never have revealed that."

I frowned because in Luckland, when someone said "one of us," they meant a true Lucklander with roots that went all the way back to the four founders. So, did Belle mean she was a descendant of one of the founders? Was she related to one of us in some way? And what did she mean by legacy? Never mind mention of Luckland's legendary gold that didn't exist except in the minds of those who came to Luckland on Founders' Day to try their luck.

"Oh, I see. I'm curious though. Did your father tell Jonathan about the, um, gold before he purchased the statue?"

"Oh my, yes," said Belle.

"Well, that *is* interesting." I stared at Devon.

"I hope it helps."

"It does, thank you." I hung up, but I wasn't sure what Belle had told us *was* helpful. In fact, I thought it added more questions to an already long list of them. Normally, I considered myself an observer. As a photographer, I captured moments. I'd only recently begun to analyze and put puzzle pieces together, and though I believed I was getting better, Devon was the master puzzler.

"Well, I didn't see that coming," I said.

"It would appear chasing after aliens would mean we're perhaps barking up the wrong tree," Devon replied.

"Or rocketing around in the wrong orbit." I shook my head. "I need a glass of wine," I said as I climbed out the car. With my brain scrambled, I needed a moment to sort through the mess.

Inside, I headed straight to my fridge, poured a glass of wine, then sat on the couch. Not surprisingly, 99 jumped on my lap, awaiting her scratches. Devon grabbed a beer from the fridge and came to sit beside me. I set my wine down on the end table and leaned into him. There was something very calming about resting my head on Devon's broad chest and listening to the steady beat of his heart. Along with 99's purrs. Not too many things kept me centered. They did.

"What do you think she meant about a Luckland gold mine?" I asked. "I mean, there's no proof anyone found gold, never mind an actual gold mine. So, why would Winston tell Jonathan Steppenhoffer about a mine?"

"I don't know, unless..."

"Unless?"

"Maybe there's some truth about the legend. Just because there has never been proof anyone found gold doesn't mean there never was any."

"You believe it's real?"

Devon shrugged. "Whether I believe it or not, obviously Winston did, and he told Steppenhoffer, who then married Prudence and convinced her aliens were real. The question is why."

"Did you notice Belle said she was 'one of us?' A Lucklander?" I asked when I'd had some time to think.

"Yes, I got the reference. In your research, did you find anything to suggest McConnell was descended from one of the founders?"

"No, but I can check. It shouldn't be too hard to do an ancestry tree. But what did she mean by legacy? She said you and I would know about the legacy. What legacy?"

"Maybe that's all linked to the founders and the gold. If McConnell is a descendant, maybe he found or knew something our mothers didn't. Maybe he was simply delusional. After all, he seemed to believe aliens had landed on Earth."

I wasn't sure. "What if Steppenhoffer thought Prudence knew something about the gold?"

"It's possible, but that would be an awful reason to marry her."

"People have married for worse," I said. I took another sip of my wine. Poor Pru. She'd had three husbands, and none seemed to have been the right man for her.

"I have a hunch, Pip," Devon said quietly. "I think some of this is connected to those damn shoeboxes you lost."

"What do you mean *I* lost? Babs sold them at the yard sale if you recall."

"Sorry, I stand corrected. The shoeboxes Babs sold."

Technically, selling the shoeboxes may have been my fault. I'd accidentally left them out during my sister's yard sale, one she was never supposed to have, and someone had marked them to sell. The boxes were supposed to be full of the family's ashes. Not secrets. However, if I hadn't left them out and they hadn't gone missing, Devon wouldn't have returned to Luckland, and he wouldn't be here with me on the couch.

"What about them?"

"If we'd found them, I doubt we'd be running around the country trying to find clues to mysteries the ladies probably already have answers to. I know they want to keep their secrets, but it's too much of a coincidence that since the boxes disappeared, Prudence's basement blows up."

"But that's to do with Elroy," I said.

"Is it? What if it's to do with something that's in those boxes? There are six of them missing, and we've worked out that whoever has them, even one of them, is threatening the ladies, but as they won't reveal their secrets, we have no idea how dangerous the repercussions might be."

I wondered again what the ladies meant when they said they were running out of time. "And you think the person who threatened the ladies blew up Pru's basement?" I wasn't so sure.

"Well, the fact no one has demanded any money doesn't bode well. Someone may be out to frighten them. Threatening phone calls, leaking recipes, blowing up a basement... What's next?"

"Then I suppose we better convene a meeting of the posse," I said. "What we've learned in New Mexico and from Belle most definitely requires some answers from that tight-lipped bunch."

"I agree. Go ahead and send out the text. Just remember, I have to get an early start tomorrow, so none of my mom's soirees, please."

I went ahead and fired off a group text with the added suggestion Hope and Marcy bring nourishment. Devon and I hadn't stopped at the store, and our food supply was semi-depleted. Pre Devon, I only shopped once a week at most. With Devon around, nothing was sacred. He was like a human vacuum. Though since he did the cooking, I gave him a pass.

After a frenzied round of texting, everyone decided we would gather at my mother's, as that was where Pru was staying for the moment. Interestingly enough, my father was there when Devon and I showed up.

"Dad, this is unexpected. You usually avoid these gatherings," I commented as we stepped out to the patio.

"My idea, Pip. I think it's best he participates a little more," my mom said, squeezing his shoulder in a show of affection.

We all gathered around the big round table. As usual, Babs left Tom at home to watch Leah. My niece was quite a handful, so it was best. Besides, Tom seemed to have no interest in the Luckland Ladies' goings-on. Hope and Marcy came through with flying colors, laying out a spread of cold cuts, freshly baked rolls, and all the fixings.

I looked at Devon seated next to me. "Well, Sherlock? Are you going to get this party started? Or shall I do the honors?"

His response was to hand me a perfectly made sandwich, accompanied by a humorous look that indicated he'd kick it off while I should perhaps eat and listen. I wasn't offended. It was his way. Besides, I was curious about his methodology. Our Roswell adventure had created a pretty convoluted scenario, what with aliens, the talk of gold mines, and disappearing spouses.

He turned to my mother. "Kate, can you tell us just a bit about the Murphy brothers?"

I glanced at him and realized he wanted to find out about the gold and the map the town's founders used to get them to Luckland, which might lead to answers about Belle's claim. My mother was a descendant of one of the original town founders, and maybe something in their story might help.

"But of course, Devon, my boy," replied Mom.

Why those women always used that phrase, I didn't know. They weren't ninety, and he wasn't seven.

My mother stood and began wandering around as she spoke. "Sean Murphy was my great-great-great-grandfather. He and his brother, Daniel, came over in 1849 during the potato famine, which, as you know, killed almost a hundred million people."

Devon tugged my braid—a reminder to let my mom speak and not correct her, although she did tend to embellish.

"They took a boat to Boston, terrible, terrible journey, which took months," she said. "Then, when they arrived, they disembarked and were immediately greeted by a distant cousin by the name of Seamus O'Connor."

"Oh yes, that was my great-great-great-grandfather," said Prudence. "Quite a handsome devil, you know."

Mom nodded, accepting Prudence's input. "Yes, Seamus approached them, and they went off to meet his friend, Logan McDonald, at a nearby tavern."

"Logan was *my* great-great-great-grandfather, and clearly, he was a handsome devil as well," Matilda said while looking at Devon.

I almost groaned. "Clearly, ladies, we are all descended from handsome devils. Perhaps we can get back to the Murphys for a moment?"

"Yes, yes, Pip, of course," my mom said. "At the tavern, other recently arrived Irishmen were scrounging coins, trying to come up with enough to purchase a pint or two. Sean and Daniel had a small amount of money. You see, new arrivals usually had their entire life savings with them. Unfortunately, it made them ripe for thievery."

"Oh, please, let me tell this part," said Matilda.

I wasn't sure how she knew what part my mother was about to tell. One of her hunches, I supposed. Matilda hopped out of her chair and joined my mother on what had become their little stage.

"Now there they all were, in a good old Irish pub, well, probably more of a slummy one, needing a good quencher, when one of the other young men held up a paper in his hand and waved it around in the air."

"Oh yes," Hope said, jumping in. "He cries out that for a mere twenty-five cents, he'll sell his treasured map leading to gold in the West."

"Seamus and Logan, of course, had no change to spare, but Sean and Daniel had a few dollars. Being the adventurous sort, they went for it."

"You mean the gullible sort, don't you?" I couldn't help it. I had to say it. Devon gave my hair another tug. I grinned at him. "Sorry."

"Perhaps you might think that way, Pippa, but here we are!" said Pru.

"Quite right, Pru," said my mom. "Here we are. They founded this wonderful town, and that is why we continue to celebrate their heroic trip across America with our Founders'

Day—which is only weeks away, you know. There are preparations to be made and rituals to be done."

With that, my mom and Matilda sat back down. Oddly, all the women shared uncomfortable glances.

"One more question, if you don't mind," Devon said. "Who are the McConnells?"

If I thought their glances were odd before, now, their expressions were downright mulish. The posse all looked as if they had no idea what Devon was talking about. Clearly, they did. It was a stare down. I looked directly at my mother because she was the one who bought half of Nadia McConnell's estate. Devon looked at Matilda, probably because he sensed she knew something. Pru and Hope exchanged another glance. Finally, it was my father who spoke up. He looked right at my mom.

"Kate, you need to tell them."

"Well, it's not as if we're trying to keep it a secret," my mom said, her tone haughty. "Daniel Murphy's grandson was Winston McConnell." She straightened her shoulders before she went back to eating as if her revelation were nothing.

"So, Nadia McConnell was a relation of ours?" I asked, wondering why trying to get information out of them was always so difficult. At least I no longer needed to research his family tree, but I wondered if they knew about Belle and her relationship to the family.

Mom sighed and turned to look at me. "Well, yes, which was why I purchased some of her estate." She glanced at Hope, but Devon stood before I could ask my mother why she hadn't said anything to me earlier.

"Okay, my turn now. Prudence, were you aware that Jonathan Steppenhoffer, your second husband, was acquainted with Winston McConnell II?"

All the women suddenly looked dumbstruck. Apparently,

our secret was bigger than theirs. Not that we were in competition.

Devon glanced at me, then turned back to the assemblage. "Were you also aware that Winston told Steppenhoffer about Luckland's alleged gold and the map?"

Eerie silence followed Devon's question, and for the very first time, the women appeared vulnerable—as if the bond they'd used all these years to fend off the outside world had been violated, which it had.

"I was played," Pru said. "He played me for a fool. Well. I've heard enough." She got up and left. Just like that. Discussion over. I looked at Devon and shook my head slightly, letting him know not to continue. Not the right time.

CHAPTER FOURTEEN

A RAW AND TERRIFYING SCREAM RENT THE AIR. DEVON, FASTER THAN the rest of us, raced around the side of the house where the scream came from. I arrived just as Devon caught a swinging bat in midair—wielded by Pru. With dusk still illuminating the sky, I spotted something on the ground. As I got closer, I could make out a familiar outline. It seemed our extraterrestrial gnome had a twin because an exact duplicate of Elroy sat at Pru's feet. Except this one still lay intact.

The women all gathered around Pru, then moved her back inside. Devon commandeered the bat, and my father went over and stood next to Devon. They looked taken aback. Oddly, I wasn't as surprised to see a second Elroy. It seemed I'd become accustomed to strange goings on in Luckland.

We headed into the house to find all the ladies talking at once. It was almost impossible to distinguish what they were saying, but it was obviously something to do with the statue.

"Can you tell me what happened out there?" Devon asked.

He must have forgotten the first rule again because they all started talking at once.

"She was unlocking her car door when she noticed a reflection in the window," said Matilda.

"She spun around, grabbed it, threw it to the ground," said Hope.

"Then she reached into the backseat where she always kept that damned bat," said my mom.

When no one else had anything to say, Devon turned to Pru. "Where was El— The statue?"

Prudence took a deep breath before answering. "The alien, you mean? Next to my car. I didn't notice it at first, but then... I thought you said it was dead." She set an accusing glare on Devon.

"This is a different one, Prudence. The other one is in a lab in Denver, where this one is going in the morning."

Prudence shook her head. "I think it put itself back together."

I didn't know if it was wise to try to explain the statue wasn't an alien. At least, I didn't think it was.

"Pip and I will take the 'statue' with us, and I think the rest of you should stay here with Prudence tonight to keep her company," Devon said. "And out of trouble." That last bit he muttered. I heard him though.

They looked at one another, then eventually nodded.

Babs cleared her throat. "Well, I must dash. Tom has a two-hour limit with Leah before he starts to go a little mad."

I sighed. I should have known Babs wouldn't hang around. She always found a way to escape when chaos ensued. As we stood and gathered our things, I noticed the rest of the women looked suspiciously expectant—as if they were anxious for us to leave.

"Dev, those women aren't just going to sit there, you know that, right?" I asked as we drove away. "You did notice their demeanor when we left."

"I'm sure they were just stunned by all the excitement."

"You don't look so sure of that." I had a hunch that he had a hunch. "Out with it. What do you think they're up to?"

"I don't know, Pip, but if I'm to be honest…"

"Yes, you must be honest. That's our arrangement."

"I think whatever it is, we're going to end up right in the thick of it," he said. Now that didn't bode well.

"Maybe if you concentrated on your intuitive powers, you'd know what it is, and we could head it off."

"I don't have intuitive powers, Pip. I'm just saying I have a hunch. That's all."

"You mean there's no logic to your powers, and you always require logic, but you're Matilda's son, so you're bound to have the same abilities she does." Made sense to me. Matilda relied on her superb sixth sense or second sight, or whatever she called it. As did Marcy, whose abilities often outshone Matilda's. They weren't always spot on, but good enough to impress. Devon shrugged off their intuition as nonsense. Like the smudge stick incident. Since I had my own share of intuitive sparks, I wasn't so quick to dismiss the possibility.

"Well, logically speaking, if I had any of Mom's 'powers,' they'd surely have shown themselves long before now."

We pulled up in front of my house, and I gazed at him. "Well, you have to admit you must have had powerful intuitive skills when you were an FBI agent. Just saying…"

He gave me a curious look as if I might be on to something, then he smiled at me, his infamous, swoon-inducing smile that meant it was time to change the subject.

We headed upstairs to focus on each other. We sometimes needed to decompress after being around the ladies, and Devon knew some great ways to reduce stress.

Monday morning arrived, along with the divine aroma of fresh coffee and the soothing chirp of birds. Devon got ready for work, and I got ready to hit the trails—if my dad would lend me his truck. Basically, back to normalcy in Luckland—if I didn't count the sound of a deafening foghorn going off in front of the house.

"Holy shit!" The words flew out of my mouth. I didn't think I had it in me to be surprised anymore, but it seemed I did.

We ran out the front door, and right there, taking up most of the street, was the biggest RV I had ever seen. Ginormous.

"What the hell is that?" I asked Devon as we stood on the porch, staring at the monstrosity that looked as if it could easily sit in the middle of a luxury RV show, with swirling spotlights and fanfare music.

The door opened like a school bus picking up passengers, with Prudence in the driver's seat. Devon and I exchanged stunned looks, which morphed into terrorized expressions when a window in the middle opened, and Matilda stuck her head out.

"Devon, my boy, we're headed out for a few days. No need to worry. I'll phone you from the road." She started to close the window when Devon stepped forward.

"Not so fast! Prudence, maybe you can shut things off for a moment and come out here?"

She turned off the engine. A few seconds later, out came not only Prudence and Matilda, but my mom, Hope, and Marcy. The posse.

"I think your hunch was pretty spot on there, Devon," I said quietly before turning my attention to the wayward women. "Just where are you all headed?"

"Just a little road trip, Pip," my mother answered. "As Matilda says, we'll be back in a few days."

As if we were going to let the ladies rip out of town in a very expensive-looking RV when aside from one little Vegas fling, they'd never been out of Colorado? From Devon's expression, it wasn't going to happen.

"Do you have a license, Prudence? To drive that thing? It requires a special kind. You know that, right?" Devon was all business now. Good tactic.

"Actually, Devon, Colorado and Arizona do not require anything special at all," she said quite glibly. Her eyes widened as she realized she'd let slip where they were going. She was still a bit loose-lipped, although she'd remained sober for the last week.

"It does require special handling, Prudence. Have you had any training?"

I'd give Devon his due. He was persistent.

"I've been training for this moment for years!" she exclaimed.

I shook my head. Letting the women go on their own could end in disaster. "Devon, we'll have to go with them. After someone blew up Pru's basement and the incident last night, we need to keep an eye on them."

Devon sighed. "I agree. We have no choice." He grabbed his phone out of his back pocket. "I'll ring Martin and let him know I'll be out of town for a few days. I'll also get him to pick up the statue and send it to the lab. In the meantime, pack a bag for yourself, and I'll keep an eye on the women to make sure they don't take off."

I headed into the house, and while there, I let Babs know she needed to come and feed and water 99. When I returned, the women were all back in the RV, seemingly ready for us to join them. I climbed on board while Devon went to pack a bag of his own.

Fully decked out with leather seating and an electric fire-place, the interior was more high-end than I'd initially thought.

However, there were bunk beds instead of a nice queen-size bed where the primary suite would generally be. The women had evidently customized this particular RV for themselves.

My mom sat with Matilda, Hope, and Marcy at the little banquette. There was a nice little sectional behind it, so I grabbed a seat there and made myself at home, curling up with my laptop and praying this monster road hog had Wi-Fi.

Devon boarded and took the front passenger seat. I presumed so he could converse with, as well as interrogate, Prudence. What she had planned involved far more than learning to handle this beast on the road. The women were up to something big. I hoped to god Devon would figure out just what that was—and, of course, to make sure it was legal.

As much as I wanted to eavesdrop, it seemed the women had other plans. The beast appeared to have an amazing sound system and a built-in karaoke. Within a few minutes, we were headed out on the open road in a forty-foot Luxmobile featuring the eighties sounds of the Luckland Ladies. Live in concert.

The intro rhythm to It's My Life, the Bon Jovi classic, filled the RV, sung by Tillie McDonald. It was going to be a long trip. If we got pulled over by some unsuspecting young highway patrol person, Devon would probably just tell them he was escorting the ladies back to their rest home. Or the New Mexico Insane Asylum. Whichever made more sense at the time.

CHAPTER FIFTEEN

The first hour of our trip wasn't easy to describe. Those women didn't just sing—they put on a fully choreographed show, which they'd probably perfected since they first became friends. That was well over fifty years' worth of belting out hit after hit, complete with dance moves.

When everyone had finally exhausted themselves, Hope and Marcy began to plan out the lunch menu. I, for one, would have been happy with just about anything, but with Devon along, lunch was a very serious undertaking. While growing up, Babs and I frequently noticed the women gave priority to Devon. Not just at mealtimes but at other times as well.

"He's a growing boy, after all," was a common phrase. "Boys will be boys," they used to say. My personal favorite? "He's just teasing."

As girls, Babs and I were not permitted any such excuses for our behavior. Even in Luckland, where women ruled the roost, those sneaky little patriarchal habits lived on.

I noticed Matilda and my mother busy studying a map on an iPad. I didn't know they had one. Perhaps it came with the beast. Everything else seemed to.

Devon quietly talked with Prudence up ahead, and I figured I could also contribute. "What are we looking for?" I asked Matilda.

"Well, there's a nice stop-off point on I-40. Before Flagstaff. Good RV parking," she said.

"Yes, and a lovely hotel as well," said my mom.

"Just out of curiosity, it seems we have plenty of sleeping room in here, so why do we need a hotel?" I thought it a legitimate question.

The women did not agree.

"Don't be silly, Pippa. We're not *sleeping* in this thing!" My mom appeared horrified at the idea.

"Oh, no," Hope said, looking up from her handwritten menu. "That would be most uncomfortable, especially for you and Devon." She had to go there, didn't she? I blushed and changed tactic.

"If nobody minds, I'm going to look around," I said to no one in particular. When I got no response, I explored the decked-out kitchen across from the sofa. With a full-size fridge, a four-burner stove, microwave, and convection oven, nothing was lacking in the culinary department. Not that I would use it, but it made sense that Hope and Marcy would require a chef's kitchen. Moving past the kitchen, I spotted a lovely restroom, though while a little small, it was well-appointed. Next up, I found another sitting area that, when parked, expanded outward. There were even little closets and a built-in hall dresser. As I headed toward the back, my mother decided to join me on my self-guided tour. I couldn't particularly say why, though I didn't mind the company. We hadn't chatted in a while, and with Devon taking up a lot of my energy lately, perhaps having a talk with her was a good idea. Mothers could come in handy every so often. I knew she had questions she wanted to ask me, though I wasn't sure I was ready to answer them.

"This is quite the people hauler, Mom. I haven't been in one like this since, well, ever. Where did you get it?"

"Well, Prudence bought it. She's been planning road trips like this for a while, and when she sets her mind on something, you know there isn't any sense trying to talk her out of it."

"I'm not saying it's a bad thing. It just seems a bit over the top, don't you think?"

"Now, Pippa, there's no such thing at our age. We don't have our whole lives ahead of us anymore, as you do. Our bucket list starts now. You understand, don't you?" She looked at me as only a mother could, which was half guilt and half *don't you dare challenge me.*

"Why now? Someone blew up Prudence's basement and tried to frighten her with an alien statue, so why would she want to plan a road trip now?"

"Never mind all that, dear. Now, tell me about you and Devon. Here, let's sit in the back. Away from prying ears." My mother was nothing if not discreet.

We headed back to what should have been the primary suite, a lovely room that now looked more like a sleep-away camp for adults. Mom took a seat on one of the bottom bunk beds, then patted the seat next to her. I wasn't sure why, but I sensed a lecture coming on. I hadn't done so much as file a single complaint about my new relationship. As far as I was concerned, things were going along just swimmingly. Yet I still had an impending sense of doom about the little chat.

"Pip, I know you think everything is just hunky-dory. I get that, but you haven't actually done this before. So, I wonder if maybe you might be open to a little advice."

"What do you mean, haven't done this before?" I hoped she

wasn't about to deliver the sex talk. "Mom, I'm almost thirty, not thirteen. You're a little late with the birds and bees thing."

"For goodness' sake, that's not what I meant. You haven't ever had any sort of long-term relationship before."

"Well, not to contradict you, Mom, but Gary from my sophomore year of college counts."

She didn't even respond. Just gave me a raised eyebrow and tipped her head.

I was grasping at straws, and we both knew it. Gary and I went out a few times that spring semester, so technically, it lasted a few months. Most of my adult life, however, had been spent serial dating. Usually at a safe distance while traveling out of the country. That way, I could return home unscathed. Having had my heart broken a time or two growing up, I'd managed to create a pretty fun and fail-safe way to protect myself. Though, looking back, I wasn't actually in love, just some heavy duty crushing on unworthy guys.

"Maybe I haven't had a long-term full-on relationship before, but that is precisely why I'm being very careful this time."

"I understand you want to be careful, but where is this relationship going?"

"I don't know where it's going, and I don't need to know."

"Oh, Pippa. Surely you have feelings for the man. Aren't you even a little bit in love with him?"

Trust her to come right down to the bare bones of my innermost emotions. I sighed. "That is a distinct possibility, yes." There. Spoken out loud. "For now, however, we're having incredibly hot and heavy sex. That's all." I ignored the heated flush on my face and hoped that would shut this conversation down.

"Pippa, dear, you might want to turn the intercom off back there," Pru said over the loudspeakers.

Oh my god, oh my god, oh my god! My life was officially over.

CHAPTER SIXTEEN

I WAS PRETTY SURE THE LOOK ON MY FACE WAS A BLEND OF SHOCK, horror, and mortification. Not even the time my bathing suit top untied in the lake at the cabin had I ever felt this exposed. In a perfect world, all would have been fine because, during that chat with my mom, Devon would have been wearing his head-phones, listening to a James Patterson audiobook. Or we'd have made a pitstop, and he would be refueling *outside*. It definitely was *not* a perfect world, however. My mother looked guilty, which she was. She knew if she hadn't brought up my love life, this fiasco I now found myself in wouldn't have happened.

"I'd say we're even now, Mom." I referred to my part in the recent accidental sale of her precious shoeboxes. I could now wash my hands clean of all guilt on that little incident.

"I'd say you are quite right, Pippa," my mom said as she leaned up and switched off the intercom. "The question is, what do we do about this?"

"I could crawl out the back window," I suggested.

"Not necessary. I have an idea." She patted my knee, her eyes gleaming.

Whatever it was, disaster loomed.

"What we need is a diversion, dear. A good old-fashioned diversion," said Matilda, standing in the doorway with Hope and Marcy right behind her.

"Well, ladies, you might as well come on in," I said, thankful the size of the RV put a lot of distance between the source of my anxiety and me. Just then, the RV shifted to the right. Prudence began to pull over—the diversion underway. I had no idea what they were planning, but I hoped it didn't involve a roadside saloon with a male strip revue. I wouldn't put it past these women.

Eventually, the RV came to a stop. When Prudence made her way to the back, I eyed her expectantly.

"What have you done with him? Is it safe to come out?"

"Oh, Pippa. Haven't we always looked out for you?" Prudence looked quite pleased with herself.

"Yes, but that doesn't actually answer my question."

"Well, if you must know, I told him the tire pressure gauge had lit up, but I wasn't sure which one. He's out there checking all of them, which should take at least twenty minutes. By then, this little breach of confidence will be just a blip on the radar for him."

"And if it isn't?"

"He will be otherwise occupied looking for an old but very dear friend in Flagstaff," my mother said in a rush.

"Yes, yes, Pippa, he will be quite focused on finding Cody," said Hope.

"Cody? I've never heard any of you mention an old friend named Cody."

"Did I say Cody? Oh, silly me," said Hope. "I meant Jody. Of course."

I shook my head. I was pretty sure they were about to send Devon on a wild goose chase to give me time to regroup. It wouldn't do any good. At best, I'd as much as admitted to being head over the moon for the guy and, at worst, using him for hot sex. Either way, I was screwed.

The women all left me alone for a few minutes, suggesting I fix myself up a bit. I glanced in the mirror and decided to let my hair down, throw on a little mascara, and swap the t-shirt for a more fitted look. If there was to be any sort of face-off, I wanted mine to be the one making him drool. I'd done it once, so I did indeed have that power over him.

I went back and sat down with Roadrunner on the couch and made myself appear busy. I hoped Devon would have the decency to simply get back on board and go back to the passenger seat next to Prudence or, even better, start driving.

I sensed the minute he started up the steps. I didn't peek at him, though it took all my willpower. Still, I could almost feel him willing me to look. I wasn't going to get sucked in that easily. I waited until I was certain he'd sat down. Certain he was busy once again. Certain it was safe.

I, oh so carefully, lifted my head and turned it ever so slightly to catch a glimpse. Like a cougar in the Serengeti, he had simply lain in wait. The minute I looked over, he winked, then grinned. Then he swiveled his chair to face the front. I breathed a sigh of relief. His wink and grin I could handle, but I was sure there'd be more, which I *couldn't* handle. I texted Dani. Dani would know what to do.

Me: Help! Ur not under the sea r u? Plz say ur not.

I didn't usually do shorthand texts, but it was an emergency.

Dani: I'm on land, no worries. What's up?

Me: Long story, will u be around tonight?

Dani: 24/7 for you, always!

Whew. That was a relief. If anyone could talk me down from the ledge on which I currently perched, it was Dani. I would just have to hold out and avoid Devon until we parked this beast for the night. At all costs, I had to avoid Devon. I didn't know how I'd make it through the next seven or so hours, which was how long I figured it would take to get to Flagstaff.

First things first, though, I needed to make it through lunch. I busied myself as the newly appointed kitchen helper, offering to do whatever Hope and Marcy needed. They weren't the most industrious café owners, so they were perfectly content to keep me busy.

Then my phone buzzed.

Babs: Where does 99 hide? I can't find her anywhere.

Though Babs wasn't the most proficient cat sitter, I didn't think she'd lose my cat on the first day.

Me: How did you lose her already? We've only been gone a few hours.

Babs: Seriously, she's not here. Ask Devon. Maybe he buried her out back.

Me: Not funny. But I will ask.

All thoughts of my humiliation flew right out the window as I jumped off the couch and basically leaped over to Devon's seat.

"99. She's gone. Babs is there now. We have to go back." I wasn't thinking of anything else past that point. I'd only had that ball of fluff for a month, and I really was quite attached to her.

Devon looked at me, tipped his head, and smiled as he reached in front of him and pulled out a carrier.

"Are you kidding me? You brought 99?"

"Guilty as charged."

"What about all her stuff? Her food, litter, treats, toys." I couldn't believe he'd done such a thing or why he hadn't told me. I'd known exactly what he was going to say next though.

"It was going to be a surprise."

Devon knew I detested surprises—unless they were the

super sweet kind. I sighed. Maybe his surprise did meet the super sweet requirements, but I couldn't let him get away with it. Just as I went to say so, he pulled out 99 and placed her in my arms. Something about holding a big fluffy, cuddly white ball of fur took the wind out of my sails.

"Okay. Truce for now, but we'll need some ground rules on these surprises." I tried to make a nice smooth exit, spinning on my heels to head back to my sofa, but the stupid welcome mat in front of the door got in my way and sent me tripping back to my seat as 99 flew right out of my arms. Much more graceful than me. Personally, I was not having a good day.

Thankfully, Hope and Marcy served lunch as I settled on the couch to lick my wounds. Since we were in motion, Devon remained at the front to dine with Prudence. The other ladies were kind enough to leave me to brood on my own. Then my phone buzzed.

Devon: Say, Red, the tests are back on Elroy and his twin.

Well, that was news. I wondered, however, if Devon telling me was just a way of distracting me from my embarrassing announcement.

Me: Do tell.

Devon: Later, but be advised, it's complicated.

Later? Was he kidding? I smelled a trap. I was sure he meant I wouldn't be able to avoid being alone with him later because the news about Elroy would be far too tempting. Saving Prudence from whatever demons were chasing her was the mission. However, Devon had pretty much become my life mission. I guess Devon was right about one thing—it *was* complicated. I just didn't think he and I were referring to the same thing.

CHAPTER SEVENTEEN

The next few hours of the trip were quite pleasant in their uneventfulness. The women got busy doing something that ultimately kept them exceptionally quiet. I peeked over the back of the banquette every so often to have a look, but whatever they were doing wasn't obvious. Not like knitting or solitaire. Their activity was more of an under-the-table kind. I could have worried about it, but at that point, why bother? I assumed it involved serious mischief. I also assumed I couldn't prevent it.

I fiddled with my photo file, scrolling through it to start narrowing down the ones that would get top billing in my blog. I had a plan that wasn't quite ready to come to fruition involving specific photos I'd taken when Devon first came back to town. He'd somehow accidentally, as I liked to say, ended up smack in the middle of them. At the time, he hadn't wanted me to post the photos, but that was because he'd been undercover with the FBI. Now, he'd given me free rein to use them, and I believed the resulting photos could help with clicks on my blog. Devon was incredibly photogenic—like the Calvin Klein underwear guy but fully dressed. My blog would go viral with him in it. While it may have been quite sexist of me, men have been using women in advertising for centuries. It was our turn now.

About to save my selection, I sensed a shadow looming. I had enough time to hit save and slap my laptop shut before Devon sat beside me.

"Guess what, Red? You won't believe it!"

He seemed excited about something, and I didn't have much room, physically or otherwise, to avoid conversing about it. Plus, I kind of liked him being close.

"Try me."

"Take a look." He handed me his iPad, though he kept it lowered so the women wouldn't see.

Geoplastic replication utilizing traditional metallurgical principles.

It was some sort of scholarly article. A very heavily redacted article, at that. One of the authors was Jonathan Steppenhoffer. The other names, I didn't recognize.

I looked quizzically at Devon. With so much of the article blacked out, I had no idea what it said. He swiped to the next tab with a photo of Jonathan and Elroy. I shrugged and raised my eyebrows. This odd sort of silent conversation was going to make me nuts.

Devon swiped again. A picture showed Jonathan in front of what appeared to be a cave-like opening. Why would an astrophysicist be spelunking? Then Devon swiped again. Another photo showed Jonathan in front of the "Welcome to Luckland" sign with Prudence standing next to him. Both sort of smiling dutifully but not very happily.

"This is very interesting, Devon. Thank you for sharing. I think perhaps we'll talk later?" I spoke aloud for the benefit of the eavesdropping women.

"Yes, I think we shall, Pip," Devon said with a wink. Then, as fast as he'd slid into my peaceful existence on the couch, he slid off and headed back to his front-row perch, leaving me to wonder just exactly what that was all about.

I couldn't get to Flagstaff fast enough, so when Pru shouted to the rest of us that we were almost there, I said a quiet little hallelujah and began to gather up my things and hunt down 99. I didn't want to spend an hour trying to get her into the carrier when we arrived. However, I couldn't find her anywhere. I ended up flat on my stomach, looking under each bunk. That was how Devon found me.

"What are you doing, Red?" I could hear the laughter in his voice.

I slithered and shimmied out from under the bed and looked up to see him standing over me, 99 all curled up in his arms.

"I was looking for 99 if you *must* know."

"Ah, then success has come to you!" He held 99 in one arm, which was no easy feat, then reached with his free hand to pull me up. I wanted to make some snappy retort, but before he headed up front, he kissed me in such a way as to leave me standing there pretty much stupefied. I seriously considered filing his lips with the patent and trademark office.

Gathering my wits, I sat down just as we pulled off the highway and peered out the window. I saw nothing at first, just some very flat land. I wondered where the mountains were. The Flagstaff I expected to see had beautiful mountains and pine forests. This little empty space had no trees. Then I saw the big sign. It appeared the posse had landed us at a casino hotel in the middle of nowhere. I really should have known. On the bright side, there was plenty of RV parking.

"I suppose there's no point in mentioning this isn't really Flagstaff?"

"Oh, we're close enough, Pip, just a half hour or so outside town. We'll have a nice meal and a nice stayover. Trust me.

You'll love it." Hope could be quite convincing at times. That wasn't one of those times. I looked at Devon to see if I could gauge his reaction. Nope. He wasn't giving a thing away.

"Well, then, ladies. As they say, let's roll!" Devon said, attempting a pun.

Matilda simply patted his hand and smiled as he helped her down the steps. As we headed inside, I noted the striking entrance. The hotel was fairly new, built by the Navajo, and thus had spectacular décor. I could do some serious shopping in the gift shop when I spotted its very impressive assortment of Navajo baskets, blankets, jewelry, and more. I mentally made plans to get some dream catchers. With all the oddities going on recently, like Elroy, the possible alien artifact, Pru's basement blowing up, and the ghostly figure of a child Devon saw on the road, it wouldn't hurt to have some protection from any ill will. Keep the nightmares at bay. Though Devon was pretty good at that too.

Checking in was simple as someone had already booked the rooms, which I assumed the women had done on the trip down here. I took the little envelope with the keycards from Matilda and headed over to the elevators.

We were all on the same floor, so as we headed to our rooms, my mother suggested we meet downstairs for dinner as soon as we had settled. It sounded like a good plan to me. Our room was spacious and modern and had every amenity including luxury robes and slippers. It would have been a nice place to relax, except we were in the middle of nowhere, babysitting the five natural wonders of Luckland.

Devon placed 99's carrier down and crouched next to it. "Now listen, 99. We could have left you on the bus to roam around, but we'd rather you stay here. Okay?" He spoke to her as he would a child—which made me smile.

"I'm afraid we may be in for an exhausting evening," I said

as I flicked through the information brochure I'd found on the desk.

"No worries, sweet pea, I have an idea."

Sweet pea?

I looked at him, then laughed as I realized he said it just to goad me. Okay. I could be a bit transparent at times. We had yet to tackle my big faux pas of the day. The time of reckoning would be at hand shortly though.

"Well, do tell. What is this stroke of brilliance?" I asked.

"You'll see. It's a sur—"

"Do not use that word. Under no circumstances." He knew what would happen if he said "surprise." Just then, my belly rumbled. "I'll forget you started to say that. Now, off we go, shall we?" I held out my arm, then smiled as he linked his with mine. We had a moment. I did love having those moments.

CHAPTER EIGHTEEN

Our practically perfect moment shattered the minute we exited the elevator downstairs and discovered exactly why we were staying in that particular hotel.

While on the RV, I'd concluded that the ladies were on this road trip as some sort of revenge plot against Jonathan. I had no idea what they intended. I didn't even know if they knew where Jonathan lived. These women, however, had tricks up their sleeves I would never have guessed, and it wouldn't have surprised me if they'd been keeping tabs on Prudence's ex. So, I assumed we were headed to Flagstaff to confront the man who made Pru believe in aliens while apparently having an ulterior motive of finding out about Luckland's alleged gold.

However, the women dressed not for revenge but for a seventies disco in sparkly, glittery, and obscenely short dresses that hugged every curve. Oddly enough, there was a seventies disco convention in that very hotel that very week. Imagine that. So once again, Devon and I misread the ladies' intentions. In a stupendously big way. It seemed the five women were out for a good time and nothing more.

Yet, a familiar sense took over. The one that told me *not so fast.* I had been taken in by the ladies' shenanigans before. I wouldn't be so gullible this time. I snuck a sidelong glance at Devon, and he nodded. Meaning he had a hunch as well. It appeared they had played us, and we'd have to play along.

"Perhaps we can get separate tables at dinner," I said, to which he simply shook his head and laughed.

According to Matilda, the casino sports bar had amazing Navajo sliders. So that was where we headed. Marcy was so impressed she ended up in the kitchen trying to get their main ingredient, the prized Navajo beef, delivered to the café. She was sure to make that happen. Meanwhile, back at our table, the women debated whether they should play slots or go for blackjack. I thought Devon and I should head off on our own and leave the others to their own devices. Regardless of how much trouble they were headed for, there wasn't anything we could do to stop it.

We excused ourselves, not that the ladies paid any attention to us, deep in a heated discussion about whether they should make this an annual trip. I wasn't sure whether they meant the seventies revival convention or the casino. Devon and I headed out into the main slot machine area, which was huge. I'd never really seen anything like it.

There were over a thousand machines of various sizes and sophistication. Some games resembled video kiosks, featuring blockbuster movie clips and really loud sirens along with what I supposed were traditional slot machines with their oranges and cherries and the number seven. I had no idea how to pick a machine. I'd read about them, but everything said there was no rhyme or reason to winning, that each calibrated machine only paid out a certain percentage using all kinds of mathematical programming well beyond any average gambler's ability to comprehend. That was where Devon would come in handy, I was sure.

"So, Dev, are you feeling lucky?"

"Oh, I certainly plan on getting lucky tonight, Red, most definitely."

I had that coming. He did, however, switch gears, his expression turning contemplative as he studied the machines. I had to admit there was an element of fun to the idea of beating the odds.

He grabbed my hand. "Let's go that way."

"Why are we speed walking?"

"Have to get to the machine before someone else grabs it," he said as if I should have known. I wondered if he'd played slots before.

I tried to guess what machine he was aiming for but there were just too many. The area was a whirlwind of lights, sound, music, and the ding, ding, ding of someone hitting it big. When we stopped, I let out a very long and loud sigh. E.T. They had an E.T. machine. Well, actually, not the real E.T. I guessed they couldn't get a license to use the trademarked icon, so the machine was a sort of cheap imitation, though still impressive with an enormous wheel up top with lights flashing everywhere and a built-in bench seat so two could play at once.

The minute we sat down, the machines transformed us from arguably competent adults to eager kids at an arcade with a few dollars to spend. Or waste. Being there reminded me of that silly claw machine that, for some reason, became a guy magnet. There wasn't a guy I knew who could resist the claw in an effort to win a stuffed animal that ended up costing a ridiculous amount of money—but it was fun.

I nicknamed the fake E.T. machine Elroy because the featured character bore a striking resemblance to him.

"Well, smarty pants, what do we do? How do you play? What's the strategy?" I asked.

"I'm not sure. I think we just put some money in and push the buttons."

"Seems a bit too simplistic. Don't you have a plan?"

"Nope." He grinned and slipped his hand behind my neck, pulling me toward him. "Kiss me for luck," he whispered. So I did. Not for luck, for me.

He slid in a twenty, and the whole machine lit up. We had to choose how much to bet, from fifty cents up to the maximum bet of three dollars.

I suggested we start conservatively. He suggested we go for broke. We settled in the middle. A dollar. That would give us twenty spins to earn our fortune. It only took one. Damn, his hunches were good. Or maybe it was the kiss.

We knew we'd done something extraordinary when the whole thing started whirring, and the screen flashed *Touch Screen Now*. We did. The big wheel lit up and started to spin as spacey music began playing. The wheel spun for what seemed an eternity. The anticipation was fun though. Devon grabbed my hand and squeezed tight while we waited. There were quite a few places the pointer could land. Several said *JACKPOT*, and above the wheel, a digital counter indicated the current jackpot was well over twenty thousand dollars.

Then the wheel stopped. I held one hand over my eyes, peeking through my fingers to see what we'd won. A whopping fifteen dollars. Fifteen smackeroos.

"Well. I guess drinks are on you, Mr. Moneybags. Nice hunch." I couldn't help laughing at how idiotic we were. I could completely understand how people got sucked into a frenzy in such places. For me, once was enough.

He laughed too. "Come on. I'll buy you a drink."

The ladies had gathered behind Matilda, seated at one of the blackjack tables. I tugged on Devon's hand, and we headed that way to see how they were faring. Hopefully better than we had. If the stack of chips in front of Matilda was any indication, she was doing just fine. Perhaps more than fine.

"I think someone is on a streak," I said.

"It would appear that way. Perhaps I need to take lessons."

"She does seem quite well versed at this game." My tone sounded suspicious, but Devon wasn't surprised.

"Quite right, Red. I think those girls' weekends at the cabin were spent differently than we imagined."

I had to laugh. I had no idea what he thought a girls' weekend was, but I was pretty sure his concept was way off the mark. Seemed mine was as well. I'd always assumed they wanted a little free time away from kids to relax, read books, and go shopping. I began to realize that was not what they did. Not at all.

We went to find a drink and ended up in what appeared to be a cross between a disco and an airport lounge. Odd but suitable for our purposes. We grabbed a table and tried to hide our amusement at the various convention-goers surrounding us. The costumes, for lack of a better word, were awesome. I counted at least five Eltons in platform shoes.

My personal favorites were the Village People. The chief wore an adapted costume that thankfully didn't include the old stereotypical headdress. The construction worker was classic—and quite hot. I grinned like an idiot when he strutted by me. Devon's expression turned ornery. I didn't think he liked the idea of me eyeing up some other guy.

"Don't worry, I don't think he's interested in me," I said, but Devon didn't look so sure.

"I saw the way he looked at you. He's only pretending to be a Village Person."

"You're cute when you're jealous." I leaned over to brush his cheeks with a kiss.

A hush fell over the room, and I held my breath in expectation. The band started with the always rousing Gloria Gaynor anthem, *I Will Survive*. The room erupted in cheers as the posse entered in a choreographed move. They loved nothing more than a grand entrance, and they paraded in as if they owned the place. Weirdly, or perhaps not, everyone in the lounge reacted as if they knew them.

I scrunched down in my seat, hoping to disappear.

Devon laughed. "Grin and bear it, Red."

"No worries. I will survive." I grinned, proud of my snappy comeback.

I would survive unless, of course, the women segued into *It's Raining Men*. Then I would have to put a stop to them, or Devon would have to put me out of my misery. So, I prayed to the disco queens that the ladies wouldn't go there.

They went there. The band began the intro to *It's Raining Men* and each of the Luckland Ladies popped open an umbrella. The table was too small to crawl under. Devon laughed so hard he had to wipe tears away. Precisely at that moment, my phone buzzed in my pocket, and I sent a silent prayer of thanks—this time to the gods of daughters everywhere for throwing me a lifeline. I slipped out to the lobby to check my messages. I was sure it wasn't important, but at that point, I didn't care.

CHAPTER NINETEEN

Me: OMG. I'm in Arizona.

Dani: Go home. I'm bringing Jake.

Me: OMG. Okay. I'll be there.

I ran back in and made a beeline for the lounge. Ignoring the ladies' umbrella dance still going on, I plopped down across from Devon.

"We have to be home by Friday," I said in a rush.

"Is this good or bad? I can't tell by your expression."

"It's most excellent news, Devon. Dani is coming home."

"She has a key, though, right?" he asked, quite oblivious to the real news.

"Of course, silly duck, but she's bringing Jake."

"Jake? The new guy?"

"Yes, her new significant other. It's critical we're there. I have to meet him and provide approval."

"I see. Is that how this works, then?"

"Of course."

"That would apply to me as well, wouldn't it? I mean, her approving of me?"

"Don't be ridiculous. She's known you for always. Now, how shall we pull this off?" I wanted assurances we could head back on Thursday at the latest.

"I'm sure we won't be staying in Flagstaff more than a few days, but if we need to, we'll just rent a car and drive back," he said.

"We could also fly back, you know. They have an airport. With planes." I was truly excited and wanted to hurry things up. I didn't get to see Dani enough, and Jake would be the first guy she had ever brought home.

A sudden breeze caused goose bumps on my arms—something was off. "Devon, my radar isn't quite as sophisticated as yours. Do you sense something amiss?"

He frowned. "No, nothing."

"Okay. So, what do you say, Peter Pan, shall we head upstairs and enter never-never land?"

He laughed as I knew he would. He took my hand, and we headed toward the elevator. Though I was ready for bed, I wasn't ready for the chat we needed. In fact, I dreaded it. I'd never publicly or privately exposed my feelings for any man, not ever, and broadcasting it on the RV intercom system was something we couldn't ignore for long.

"Oh, Devon, Pippa, there you are!" Matilda barreled toward us with the rest of the gang right behind. So much for never-never land.

"Spectacular night, don't you think?" she asked as she approached.

"I think, perhaps, the Luckland Ladies have been quite lucky tonight," said Devon. "I was hoping to get lucky myself. It seems that's not in the cards." His attempt at humor was, at times, completely inappropriate, and a flush rose to my neck and face, clearly indicating he should stop. Instead, he leaned close.

"I'm thinking I'll have more luck upstairs, however," he whispered in my ear.

Unfortunately, my mother's hearing was extraordinary. Like a super spy bug.

"Devon, I might remind you that Pippa is my daughter, and as much as I appreciate your appreciation of her, you might keep those thoughts to yourself."

Things were completely going off the rails, so, in my most polite voice, I excused us, grabbed his arm, and tugged him away from the prying ears and eyes of the posse.

"Come on, let's go while you still have all your limbs attached."

Once in the elevator, he kissed me, perhaps to erase the sound of my mother's voice in my head—or the sound of mine on that damn intercom.

We stepped off the elevator, and Devon stopped short. On full alert, he put a finger to his lips, signifying I should stay quiet. Since Devon on full alert terrified me, I stayed quiet and perfectly still. He reached down and slipped a revolver out of his boot. Shocked, I wanted to ask how he brought the gun in with him. I was pretty sure the sign on the main door said no weapons. Then again, he was a cop, and I didn't know the rules of what they were and weren't allowed to do.

He put up his hand—the silent don't move sign, then began to head toward our room. Going past it, he headed to Pru's room next to ours. It was then I noticed the partly open door. We'd just left Pru downstairs.

I should have told Devon not to dare enter that room, that he should call security. Instead, I watched him nudge the door with his foot and pause.

After a moment, he stepped into the room, and I had to decide to either stay still or tiptoe closer. What if we were followed and whoever blew up Pru's basement was trying to blow up her room? I should warn him. I took two steps forward, stopped, took another two, then waited. I repeated the process a few times, worried my new boyfriend might die. Well, maybe not die, but he was certainly, possibly, in mortal danger.

When I got halfway there, he reentered the hallway and sighed in consternation.

"Perhaps you could text the ladies to come upstairs if they aren't on their way, Red. Make yourself useful?"

The elevator doors opened just at that moment, and out the ladies came. They looked so happy I hated to see Devon burst their bubble, but he'd have to tell them something since he stood in front of Pru's open door.

"Devon, isn't that my room, or do I have the wrong number?" Prudence checked her key envelope.

"Sorry, Pru, but your door was open when we got up here. It's all clear, but I'm a little concerned. Unless you forgot to close the door earlier?"

"No. I closed it and made sure it was snug and tight." Her hands shook, conveying her nervousness.

"Then I suggest we all collect our things and head back to the RV," said Devon.

Without protest, everyone gathered their belongings. I grabbed 99, then we all headed out to the RV.

"Devon, what if someone also broke into the RV? Shouldn't we call security?" I asked in a whisper so as not to alarm the women. However, they all chattered so much behind us, I doubted they'd have heard.

"I'll check it out first, and I did call security while in Pru's room. They said to let them know if there were any more issues. Don't worry, but you stay here," he said as we approached the beast. "I mean it, Red. Stay put."

His emphasis was a tad unnecessary. I must have annoyed him more than usual in the hallway, or he was genuinely concerned for my safety. So, I waited with the other women, who all seemed oblivious to any danger that might lurk in the RV. It was as if they compartmentalized everything, and when they were all together like that, they had an invisible shield that warded away danger.

After going aboard and checking inside, Devon crouched to inspect the vehicle's undercarriage using the high-powered flashlight from the RV's emergency toolkit.

"Okay, we're good to go. All aboard ladies!" A bit of humor threaded his voice, so I assumed all was well.

We climbed aboard, and the women headed straight for the back, where the bunks were.

"Devon, did you discover anything from Pru about why they were going to Flagstaff?" I asked in a whisper.

"Nope, she wouldn't tell me. Why don't you see if you can find out anything."

"I don't think they'd be any more willing to talk to me."

"Well, they did tell you about the Vegas millions and that someone was trying to blackmail them." He smiled as if to say he trusted me to gain the women's confidence. His trust was poorly placed, but I headed to the back, full of questions—then stopped when their hushed voices filled the space between us.

"We'll have to send them back."

"First thing tomorrow."

"Yes, why don't you book them a flight."

"It was him. We all know it. It's time."

"Agreed?"

"All for one and one for all!"

CHAPTER TWENTY

"The question is, who is 'him'?" I asked Devon as we waited for our flight to take off. "I'm sure it's Jonathan, but we need to find out for sure. I think they're up to no good."

"Clearly, they're up to no good. So yes, we need to know."

"You're a bit grumpy this morning," I said. "What's got you in such a snit?"

"Other than the fact the posse took off without us?"

While we were all inside the casino getting breakfast, the ladies disappeared. A few minutes later, my mom sent a text telling us to check the front desk. When we did, we found airplane tickets, our bags, and 99 waiting for us. After the ladies' whispered conversation, Devon and I had figured the ladies intended to get rid of us while they continued to who knew where or why. Devon thought he could outsmart them by taking the RV keys. Seemed they had a spare set.

"Yes. Other than that. You are not your usual charming self."

"If you must know, they've done it again. It's that simple," he said.

"Done what?"

"They sent us home like the kids they think we are. Must they always dictate our lives? Do they ever stop to think? I mean, do they?" He really was put out.

"Considering they recently bought us a house, this is minor league in comparison."

Devon still looked tense, so I smiled and hoped it conveyed my empathy.

He shook his head and frowned. "You don't understand. You've been living with these women your whole life. Totally under their thumb. I, on the other hand, have been independent for the last decade. I am now the chief of police. Do you think you could all give me just a little control over my life?"

There were so many things wrong with that particular speech.

"*All?* Are you including me with them? So, *I'm* the problem? I'm just like *them?* Is that what you're saying?"

He studied my expression, probably trying to gauge whether he'd stepped into a rabbit hole. No, he hadn't stepped into a rabbit hole—he'd fallen all the way down to the bottom.

"Look, sometimes you get caught up in their schemes, but maybe you could be on my side every now and again," he replied, his voice quiet and a little hesitant.

"Here's how it is. I'm going to put everything you said aside and let you think about it. Really and truly think. Eventually, I might forgive you for being a jackass." I turned away from him, fiddled with my seatbelt as we were now landing, and readied myself to jump out of the seat and grab my bag along with 99, who'd been sleeping blissfully in her carrier.

Devon and I would have to ride back together to Luckland, but he was definitely in the doghouse as far as I was concerned. After the fiasco with the intercom the day before, and knowing how incredibly vulnerable I felt, Devon had the audacity to pull the put-upon guy act. I'd seen it before from others. The minute they realized I had any sort of feelings for them, they tried to control the relationship. Worse, they tried to control me. Not happening.

We grabbed a rental car and spent the next hour in silent tension. As we finally pulled up my driveway, I opened the car door. "Don't bother getting out," I said, a bite to my words. "You'll be staying with your *mother* until further notice. How's that for control?"

His face took on a distinctly pallid look. "I'm sure we can talk this out, Pip," he said quietly.

"Nope. I'm going to need some space. You understand space, don't you?" Though I had already begun creating a checklist in my head for what he'd have to do to earn my forgiveness, right now, I had to put myself first. I got out with 99's carrier and my bag. I didn't look back.

He waited in the driveway for a while before heading out. I watched him through the blinds until he'd gone, then I went into the kitchen and brewed a giant mug of good coffee before I sat down in *my* recliner, 99 in my lap, to contemplate not just the Devon thing because that would right itself eventually, but who was trying to frighten Prudence. I had a feeling Jonathan had something to do with it, and the ladies thought the same thing. My initial belief that they had gone to Arizona to exact revenge on Jonathan still seemed a likely scenario considering they'd gotten rid of Devon and me so they could continue their trip, but what the women had in mind, I had no idea. I contemplated calling my mom to ask what they were up to, but I doubted she'd answer the phone, and even if she did, she probably wouldn't tell me their plans.

There were a lot of questions surrounding Prudence, like what had happened to her first husband and why she'd bought the astronomical map from Winston. Devon should have asked her about the map when he rode up front with her in the RV, and for all I knew, he'd gotten some answers but hadn't had a chance to let me know what they were. So, I needed to talk to Devon if I had any chance of sorting out what was going on. Well, damn. I was not, however, going to grovel or ask him to come back.

Edgy, I got up and paced. I needed a distraction. Dani wouldn't arrive until Friday, so I had to do something with myself in the meantime. With a sigh, I decided to go to the shop and check in with my dad. There might even be some new arrivals I could catalog. That would certainly keep me busy. First, I opted to pop by and see Babs. Luckily, she was almost always home, even when working on her new interior design business.

Upon arriving, I rapped the knocker as the doorbell just wasn't annoying enough for me, and the door opened almost magically. I looked down to see Leah grinning at me as if she'd mastered the best skill ever. Babs had to be behind the door, which was made of heavy oak. No way that child opened it. I played along anyway, earning me a great big hug around my knees. She tried to drag me down like the *Boncos*, as she called them. I was pretty sure she meant Tom's favorite football team.

"To what do we owe the honor, Pip?" Babs asked. "I thought you were babysitting Mother and her gang of thieves." She'd been calling the ladies that since she learned they found a bag of millions in Las Vegas and didn't give it back.

"Well, the ladies got tired of our company and sent us home," I replied.

"So, where's hot stuff?"

"Hot stuff? Just who might that be?" She meant Devon, but I needed to vent some anger.

She smirked. "Devon, your boy toy."

"I don't know. He's off doing whatever arrogant cops do when trying to establish their superiority, I suppose."

"Oh, Pippa, please tell me you haven't let him get the upper hand, have you? No, no, you wouldn't. What did he do? Is it just a little spat? Or do we need to shun him?"

Now there was the Babs I knew and loved. We didn't always agree. Mostly never, but we did stick up for each other.

"Well, Mom bought plane tickets to send us home and left them at the hotel's reception desk while Devon and I were having breakfast. Devon didn't say a word at the time, but on the plane, he said plenty. Remember when they bought the house, and he got all huffy? Well, same thing. Only this time, he implied I was just as bad as them. I'm trying to control him now, it seems."

"Well, then, he'll have to pay. He'll need to learn. This is Luckland, after all. He ought to know better. Why don't you come with Leah and me? We're off to the salon for a much-needed pedicure." Babs had Leah get pedicures because the whole idea of clipping her daughter's nails gave Babs the willies.

"While the idea sounds minimally appealing, I'm going to the shop. I'll take a rain check though."

After giving Leah a hug goodbye, I drove over to the store, parked out back, then went in to find my dad sitting up front with a book. I gave him a quick hug. It wasn't until then I realized how much I needed hugs after the way Devon had lumped me in with the manipulative women. I wasn't anything like them, and Devon needed to realize that. Fast.

"Whatcha reading?" I peered over his shoulder. "Oh, TK Moreaux, good one." My favorite mystery author. "I'll borrow it when you're finished."

"You should buy your own copy. Authors need the royalty."

I smiled because he was right. There was a whole industry behind books, and everyone deserved their due.

"So, have you heard from Mom?"

Dad shook his head. "Not a word since this morning."

"Hmm. Okay, well, I thought I'd update the website and catalog any new stock."

Dad waved at a couple of new boxes, and I headed to take a look. Much of the contents seemed pretty routine, interesting enough but nothing that made the hair on my neck stand up. I grabbed a huge, overstuffed pillow and placed it on the floor so I could relax with Roadrunner. I used to sit in one of the large throne chairs we'd kept in the store, but a pair of newcomers to Luckland had recently purchased them. As it turned out, the newcomers were criminals who were now behind bars, but we didn't yet have the chairs back.

I fired up Roadrunner and began researching each piece. Dad went off to scrounge us up some lunch at the café, and when he returned, I'd made significant headway. We took our little picnic outside and sat on the back patio, where my mother had set up a little outdoor retreat with a pair of wicker chairs, a tile-topped table, and a few potted plants. It wasn't the garden of Eden, but it was sufficient for us to relax.

"So, Pip, what happened this morning? Your mom said you'd decided to come home early."

"No. Mom and the glee club gang got tired of us hanging around and sent us home. Did you know about the RV and the trip?"

"Well, I knew about the RV. Not the trip until yesterday, but they've been planning to go on one for a while."

"Any reason nobody told the rest of us? The first thing I knew about that monstrosity was when they pulled up in front of my house, blaring the horn."

"The RV was meant to be a surprise," he said, chuckling.

Dad knew about my strong aversion to surprises that began with a stupid tin box with a handle my parents cranked until a clown popped out and scared the bejesus out of me. Yet everyone seemed to want to surprise me anyway. Granted, I accepted their surprises were a kind of twisted and perverse way of showing they all cared about me.

Devon chose that moment to pull into the lot. I smiled. Not the *happy to see Devon* kind. My smile was more devilish because if he was there to apologize, I looked forward to making him squirm first.

Confident he'd follow, I gathered my things and headed inside. However, after more than half an hour, neither my dad nor Devon came in. I frowned, wondering if Devon was seeking advice from my dad or if Devon had simply left and gone about his business.

Frustrated because I wasn't getting a darn thing done, I was just about to give up and head back outside when I spotted a small but ornate box I'd never noticed before, sitting on the windowsill.

The top of the silver box was almost three-dimensional with a carved relief that looked like planets in orbit around a sun. At first, I thought the box was quite old, but then I noticed it had nine planets. I didn't know all that much about astronomy, but I did know Pluto was only on the map since the twentieth century and had recently been downgraded to a dwarf planet at that. So, if the box was from the nineteenth century, it should only have had eight planets. I assumed my dad could figure that out, so I placed it aside. Then, having second thoughts, I decided to go ahead and open it. I knew to be extra careful as old latches were quite thin and could bend easily with too much pressure. Opening it up, I gasped, then rushed out the back, box in hand.

As soon as I stepped outside, Devon stood.

"Pippa, can we talk?"

"Not now, Groucho. Your apology will have to wait," I replied, almost bouncing on my toes.

"Apology? I'm not going to apologize," he grumbled.

"Oh, you most certainly are, but right now we've got bigger fish to fry. Take a look!"

CHAPTER TWENTY-ONE

I held the open box out in front of them, and as the sun hit the underside of the lid, they gasped. I certainly had their attention because right there on that very underside of the lid was a sketch of Elroy. I'd never seen anything like it, and apparently, neither had my dad nor Devon. Devon reached out to take the box from my hands, but I quickly clutched it to my chest.

"Oh no, finders keepers. You are not taking this box from me," I said in my nicest, super sweet voice—with a little snark for good measure.

"Might I remind you, Pip, I am the chief of police around here."

"No crime has been committed. This item belongs to the shop. I'm adding it to our inventory, and you can examine it further when I'm done." I spun around and headed straight back into the store. He still owed me an apology. I hadn't lost sight of that, but this box was the start of something big. I knew it. I was sure the whole sordid tale of Elroy would finally come together. Maybe.

I took a few photos of the box, uploaded them, then began an image search. I hoped to find a box just like it. Eventually, I found the one I was looking for among the hundreds of images of old silver boxes similar in size and shape. I clicked on the image and zoomed in, then clicked the link to the website the image came from—the International UFO Artifact Society. I didn't believe in coincidences, just like Devon, and the box turning up in our shop mere days after seeing images and statues of Elroy all over the place was too much of a coincidence as far as I was concerned. Something was at play. I just didn't know what.

I could have waited for Devon before going any further, but when I got my mad on, it took a while to let go of it. So, I called Belle Chantelle.

"Belle, it's Pippa. I found an image on your website of a small silver box with some planets carved on top. Do you remember it?"

I didn't bother with pleasantries. I needed facts.

"I do. Funny enough, that was a piece Jonathan bought years ago."

"I see. Well, I just fell in love with it, is all." My gut told me not to tell her I had the box because she answered far too quickly. She didn't even need to look it up, and once again, her familiar use of Jonathan's name caught my attention.

"Yes. It would certainly suit your little antique shop. So, was there anything else?" Belle asked.

I didn't remember telling Belle about the antique shop, but I guessed I must have. "Oh. No, thanks. Bye." I hung up.

I wasn't sure if I should tell Devon what I'd learned. I had no idea if the box had anything to do with Prudence's home explosion and who left the second Elroy beside her car, but it seemed likely. There was also the question of how the box ended in our shop. As far as I could tell, there was no paperwork. Also, my dad hadn't seemed to recognize it. I frowned, then decided to wait until I did some more investigating.

I packed up my things, including the box, and headed to my car. Devon stood on the back porch, but I simply barreled right past him. He didn't try to stop me. It would have been pointless, but he should have tried. How could someone charged with solving crimes be so dense?

After I arrived home, I cracked open a nice fruity Moscato, sat at the kitchen table with Roadrunner, and began a new file on Elroy. I collected all the images I had and all the linked sites they came from, then I typed up a brief history of what we knew regarding the strange life of the alien gnome. I briefly considered joining a forum with some sci-fi buffs, but I didn't think Elroy was the main focus—he was just a decoy, but a decoy for what?

I sat back and reviewed my summary.

Prudence married a guy named Wally, who went berserk and vanished, leaving her alone, confused, and with Elroy in her trunk. Two years later, she married Jonathan, who at one time had custody of Elroy and the box. Both of which he'd purchased from the UFO society. Why? Had he truly believed in alien artifacts? If so, why had he either given Elroy to Wally or directly put the statue in Prudence's trunk? The other question was why he had tried to get Prudence to believe in aliens. I still believed Steppenhoffer thought Prudence knew something about Luckland's legendary but unproven gold. Devon had also thought the same. To think the professor had caused Prudence all that pain and confusion because of greed had me angrier than a disturbed hornet's nest.

I needed Devon right about then, but I needed my pride more, so I did what anyone else would do; I fixed myself a toast and jelly sandwich, had one last glass of wine, watched a few episodes of Will & Grace, then went to bed. Unfortunately, I couldn't sleep. With Devon in my life, my insomnia had seemed to magically disappear. With him at Matilda's, sleeplessness was back with a vengeance.

After a fabulous night of tossing and turning, dawn light slipped around the shades just as my phone began to buzz like a chainsaw. I smacked around the top of my nightstand until I found the phone and squinted to read the screen.

A text. From my mother. My mother? She rarely texted me unless something were terribly wrong. My stomach sank.

Mom: Come quickly.

I answered, but it took a few tries.

Me: Home there! Wave the flag!

Damn autocorrect. Eventually, my fingers cooperated.

Me: Come where? Aren't you in Flagstaff?

Mom: Pulling into my drive. Hurry.

I tried to figure out how they were already home. They must have left last night, but why? I threw on some sweats and barreled over there, wondering whether they'd also invited Devon.

To my relief, it seemed they hadn't. I let myself in and found them all in the kitchen, bustling about making coffee, unloading bags of food into the fridge, and talking over one another.

I stood in the doorway and waited to see if they'd notice me. To my chagrin, they hadn't. I was about to call attention to my presence when a faint thumping started beneath my feet. Startled, I glanced down. The knocking definitely came from the floor. From the basement. Looking back up at the women, I wondered if they heard it too. Then my chest tightened when I realized they might be chattering to cover it up.

"Mom!" I yelled. "Hey, Mom!"

They all stopped and looked at me.

"There appears to be something thumping in the basement. Care to explain?" When the ladies just looked at one another, I took a risk. "Anyone?"

"Well, that's just the thing, Pippa," said my mother. "We might have brought back a souvenir. An unwilling one."

A what? When I woke up that morning, I never would have guessed how my day would turn out, but maybe I should have. "Should I be terrified?" Looking from one to the other, I suspected the answer was yes. They all appeared quite nervous, glancing at one another for support.

"Did anyone bother to notify Devon that we have a situation?" I knew that would get them talking. I was right.

"Oh, my goodness. That would be a terrible idea," said Matilda.

"Quite right, Tillie," said Hope.

"I think we need to handle this ourselves, Pippa," said my mother.

"Perhaps you need to see for yourself," said Prudence.

Nope. Whatever the women were up to, we needed more than just "we" to handle it. I needed reinforcements. "Maybe we should have Babs come over."

"Yes, yes, she's on her way," said my mom.

Relieved, I sat down and waited. The thumps continued, and I couldn't help wondering what was causing them. Was it an alien? An escapee from the nearby wildlife refuge? A spirit out to do some harm that they'd managed to trap? My mind could conjure up some amazing scenarios in such tense and bizarre situations. Thankfully, my sister arrived quickly. She sat at the table with me, and all the other women followed suit. Marcy poured coffee for everyone and served it up with some fabulous scones. Even with a thumping creature in the basement, the women were proper hostesses.

"So, what's the emergency?" Babs asked in naïve wonder while she looked at me.

"Seems they have a houseguest. In the basement," I said.

"And?"

I shrugged and expectantly looked at my mom, who looked at Prudence, who stood and nodded at everyone. Sometimes, I wondered if we were all actors in some sort of reality show they'd been constructing for years. It started to feel that way.

"Jonathan is in the basement," announced Prudence.

CHAPTER TWENTY-TWO

Being the accidental spitter, it was a very good thing I hadn't anything in my mouth at the time.

"Beg pardon?" asked Babs.

"What Pru is saying is that her former husband, the snake, is in the basement," said Hope.

"Getting back to the unwilling part, if I may, can I assume the thumping is his way of expressing displeasure of some sort?" I asked.

"Well, most likely, that would be correct," replied my mother. "Would you like to meet him?"

I didn't, to be honest. What I would have liked at that moment was Devon. As mad as I was at him, there were times in life we all needed someone to lean on, and I, for one, had no intention of going down to that basement with the posse. I was sure Babs felt the same.

"I'm going to pass on that, Mom, for now," I replied. "I will, however, take another scone."

Babs stared open-mouthed as the ladies began chatting again about what they should do with their prisoner. I tuned them out and focused on alerting Devon. He'd installed a nifty app on my phone that I tapped in case of emergency, and he came to the rescue. I'd only used it once when the Panello brothers held us females at gunpoint. I sure hoped the app would work once again. I also hoped Devon didn't burst through the door like a maniac.

I nodded to Babs, signaling I had things under control. By then, everyone sat in relative silence, listening to the thumping from below, until Babs began tapping her fingers in a nervous gesture. I couldn't blame her because having a prisoner in my mother's basement was nerve-racking. My mind raced with the image of Jonathan duct taped to a chair, hopping up and down, trying to get to the door—unless they'd shackled him to the wall. Once I'd envisioned that, I couldn't unsee it.

About five minutes passed before a knock sounded at the door. The ladies became very quiet.

"Is someone going to answer that?" I asked.

"Don't be silly. It's probably Devon or Martin, and they can't come in!" exclaimed Prudence, a trace of panic in her voice.

Deputy Martin? Devon, I expected, but why would Martin come around so early in the morning?

"Well, I would think it's far more suspicious not to answer the door with all our vehicles sitting out front. It's obvious someone is here," Babs said.

"True, so I'm going to answer the door," said Matilda. "Everyone hush up."

I leaned forward in my chair, quite intrigued. I couldn't see the front door from the kitchen, so I listened closely.

"Hello, Devon, my boy. What brings you here?" Tillie asked, far louder than necessary.

"Mom? I saw the Jeep and the RV... I was simply looking for Pippa. Do you know where she is? Also, how are you back?"

Devon sounded quite sincere, almost totally believable—as if I hadn't summoned him with the emergency app.

I waited to see if Matilda would admit I was there or not.

"Oh yes. Pippa was just stopping by for a scone. I'll tell her you're here." She didn't answer his question about how or why they were back.

"You aren't going to let me in?" Devon asked. "Can't I have a scone as well?"

I hid a grin. There was no way Matilda could say no to him.

"Well, I suppose just one scone wouldn't hurt. Come in, then. Be quick about it though."

Curiously, my mother made a beeline over to the wall intercom and pushed a few buttons. I about flew out of my chair when the speaker system in the house started blaring the soundtrack to Saturday Night Fever. Nice move. The heavy bass track would hide the thumping from below.

Devon followed Matilda into the kitchen and sort of stopped to lean against the wall. He nodded hello to all the ladies in a very brusque manner. I sensed he was still quite annoyed with all of them. Well, all of *us*. Then he focused on me. Laser beam focus. With his expression a combination of heat and sweet, it almost succeeded in melting my resolve. Almost. I had the will of a lion, however, and he wouldn't break me that easily.

Since I did need his help, I gave him just a hint of a smile— the kind he could interpret in a whole host of ways. A trick I'd learned from Prudence. She was my mentor in the boy department growing up. She made the most of her feminine wiles and had tried to pass her tactics along to me. As I learned more about her past, however, I realized there was so much more to her than the inebriated vivacious flirt with an active social life I'd always known.

Marcy handed Devon a mug of coffee and a plate of scones,

then began ushering him out to the patio. My mother looked at me and nodded toward the door, silently urging me to go with him. So, I did, knowing that to save us all from impending doom, I'd be making the ultimate sacrifice and giving in to him before his big apology. I'd have to tread carefully.

Once outside, with the door closed, I figured it was safe to talk.

"Full disclosure, they told me that Jonathan is in the basement," I said.

This time, Devon spat out his coffee. Luckily, away from prying eyes.

"What the hell?"

"They don't want you to know. I'm violating the sacred pact by telling you. What you do with this knowledge is up to you. I'm going inside now, and we will pretend we never had this conversation."

I didn't wait for him to reply. I simply went back inside, closed the door behind me, and headed back to the kitchen, where they stared at me. I also noticed it was quiet again. No music. They couldn't have known I ratted them out. Or could they?

"Pippa, how could you?" asked my mother.

"How could I what?"

"The intercom, Sis," Babs replied. "It seems you've recently gotten into the habit of blabbing on intercoms."

Babs appeared to actually enjoy my discomfort. I swallowed hard as I realized the ladies had flipped the switches the minute I went outside. I really should have known better.

The back door opened, but I didn't bother turning around. Devon set his cup and plate on the table, then rested his hands on my shoulders. I looked up at him, and he must have noticed my expression. I guessed I looked mortified. I had just ratted out my mother and her friends, and they knew it. Not my finest hour.

"What did I miss?" Devon asked in his most innocent voice.

"Well, Devon, it seems the RV isn't the only place around here with intercoms," Babs said.

He looked down at me, then at the women. "I see. Well then, why don't I go down and see what's in the basement? Or should I say, who?"

"Before you do that, there are a few things we might not have mentioned," Matilda said as she pulled out a chair and indicated he should sit. "You need to know everything."

Devon sat, then pulled the other chair out for me, so I sat as well. He squeezed my hand, which I thought was more to reassure himself than to reassure me, but perhaps he truly understood the sacrifice I'd made in sharing the ladies' secret.

The rest of the women grabbed a seat as well, and we all waited as Prudence, once again, took center stage.

"It's Jonathan's fault that Teddy is dead," she said. "Teddy was my third husband, and while he was a bit of a jackass, he didn't deserve to die that way."

"What way was that, Pru?" asked Devon.

"Teddy got run over by the garbage truck. He'd forgotten to put out the trash can and ran right out into the street in front of the truck while holding up a prototype for a device that was supposed to instantly make people stop in their tracks and obey any command."

"And what role did Jonathan play in all this?" Devon asked.

I was still stuck on the device, but perhaps if I heard the rest...

"Teddy told me that Jonathan gave him the device. I asked Teddy about it when I saw it on the dresser one day. He said he went to one of Jonathan's lectures and met him afterward, and Jonathan told him NASA had originally developed the device to control aliens who'd already arrived here, but it also worked on people. I assumed Teddy had wanted the truck driver to stop and thought the device would make him."

Devon frowned. "And how is that Jonathan's fault?"

Pru tutted. "Well, if Jonathan hadn't given Teddy the device, Teddy would still be alive, wouldn't he?"

Matilda shook her head. "We don't believe the device was real or there are aliens on Earth. It's all a big lie and a scheme of Jonathan's, but we can't convince her otherwise."

After meeting with Belle and hearing her stories about the asylum and Roswell, I wasn't sure if aliens on Earth were a hoax. Who was to say?

"Prudence, can I ask just how many husbands you've had?" I knew of Wally, Jonathan, and the third husband, who she said was Teddy, but were there more?

"Just the three, sweetie, that's all." She smiled, seeming almost relaxed. Perhaps having Jonathan hog-tied in the basement allowed her to breathe easy for the first time in decades. Maybe.

"I think I understand it all now, and it's time we meet Jonathan." Just like that, Devon seemed to have the answers.

I wasn't sure, but I also thought I had it figured out. I'd have to see if his hunch was better than my logic. "I think I know too. In fact, I'm sure of it," I said.

He looked at me, grinned, and tugged on my braid. Maybe it gave him good luck.

"What do you say, ladies? Shall I go and see what lies beneath?"

CHAPTER TWENTY-THREE

We all followed him to the basement door, where he quite
suddenly turned and held up his hand. He looked at each of us,
his gaze stern.

"I'm going down alone. Are we clear?"

I checked around to see if anyone was listening. It appeared
they were, but they were all glancing at one another—having
one of their silent conversations they'd mastered over the last
fifty plus years.

"I'll call if and when I'm ready for you to come down," he
said as he turned and headed downstairs.

I followed him.

He stopped midway and turned to stare me down. "Pippa,
you have to wait up there," he whispered.

Wild thumping saved me from having to argue. Our victim
must have heard Devon's voice and thought someone had come
to rescue him. Devon turned his attention to the unwilling
guest, and I continued to follow, one hand on Devon's back as
he hadn't switched on the light. I wasn't going to miss any of
the action, especially since I was pretty sure the professor was

unarmed, and I knew Devon packed a pistol in his boot. In fact, as we approached the bottom, he retrieved his gun. If I knew those rabble-rousers upstairs, their victim wasn't going anywhere or harming anyone. Though I imagined the danger was always there after kidnapping someone.

When we reached the bottom of the stairs, Devon flipped the switch and flooded the unfinished basement with light. Seated right in the middle was the professor wrapped up like a silver mummy, with duct tape wound around and around his body and the chair. They'd taped his mouth but hadn't covered his eyes, which were as wide as saucers as he threw his body from side to side. The chair legs banged against the concrete floor each time. Thump. Thump.

I didn't move, mesmerized by the horrifying yet fascinating sight. Devon slipped his gun into the waistband of his jeans, then stepped toward our victim. I continued to shuffle behind him until he stopped about two feet from Jonathan.

"Do you speak English?" Devon asked, his tone professional.

Jonathan nodded. Pretty clever of Devon to imply we had no idea who Jonathan was.

"I'm Police Chief Marks."

Jonathan nodded again, a little less freaked out now.

Devon strode to the chair, then patted one side of Jonathan's body before striding to the other side and repeating his search. It was awesome to see Devon in action.

"I'm going to get you out of here. Before I peel off this tape, I'm warning you. You will do exactly what I say. Do you understand?"

I didn't think I'd ever heard him sound quite so forceful. Incredibly hot to witness.

"Let's get some of this tape off, shall we?" He then grabbed one end of the tape covering Jonathan's mouth, yanked, and ripped off that sucker.

A yelp of pain erupted from Jonathan, which he totally deserved.

Devon grabbed a folded pocketknife from his pocket, then flicked it open with one quick gesture. Very impressive.

"I'm going cut you loose, but you're not going to move. Are we clear on that? I need to ask a few questions. First and fore-most, I'll need your name."

"Professor Jonathan Steppenhoffer," he replied in a very snooty manner.

Devon began cutting the tape from Jonathan's legs, leaving him still pretty well tied to the chair.

"Okay, Professor, how did you end up in this room?"

I took a step closer because I was sure whatever the professor said, it had to be good.

"I don't know, precisely." He shook his head, his voice quiet. "I was in the observatory, mapping a new star system, and when I awoke, I was riding in some vehicle with horrible music blasting, all taped up like this. My head is pounding. I assume I was struck."

"How did you get from the vehicle to here?" Devon asked. "Were you still awake?"

"Yes, but someone had blindfolded me, and they roughly dragged me down here. I have no idea who it was. They didn't say a word, but they kept pulling my hair. It was quite painful."

"I see," said Devon. "Do you have any enemies that you know of?"

"No, of course not. I'm a research scientist. Nobody cares a whit about what I do."

"Ever married?"

Oh, goodie... I took another step closer.

"No," Jonathan replied—again in that snooty tone.

What an interesting answer. Now it was getting really good. Obviously, he was lying to Devon, which meant Jonathan was no innocent. That meant maybe Devon wouldn't have to arrest our moms for kidnapping.

"Where is this observatory you spoke of?" I asked.

"Lowell. I've been conducting research there for years." He looked from Devon to me as if confused. "Aren't we in Flagstaff?"

"Afraid not, Professor. Looks as if you traveled far from home," Devon replied as if it were no big deal. However, he had a gleam in his eye, and his jaw twitched—a clear sign he was about to go in for the kill.

"How do you know Prudence Smalley, Professor?"

Devon didn't ask *if*. He asked *how*.

"Pru? Haven't seen that madwoman in years," Jonathan said, all huffy. "You think she's involved? I wouldn't put it past her. Crazy as a loon, that woman."

Well... That was all it took. The door at the top of the stairs burst open, and down flew Pru with the rest not far behind. The intercom. Devon didn't even flinch.

Jonathan tried to jump up even with his arms and torso still taped to the back of the chair. He ended up flipping the whole chair over with him in it. Nobody moved to help.

Devon just stared at him. Then, with a cold voice, he said, "I told you not to move."

"Well, Jon, what do you have to say for yourself now? Hmm? Hmm? Never married? I'm a madwoman? Tell Devon about them. Go on, tell him!"

Matilda and my mom held on to Pru to keep her from Jonathan. I had a feeling she would have ripped into him, more than likely kicking him while he was on the floor.

"Shut up, you crazy woman. You belong in the asylum. You know it, and I know it." He was a vicious one—and nervy, all taped up and insulting her like that.

"You know, I don't believe we have asylums anymore, and if we did, you'd probably be first in line," I said. Devon raised his eyebrows at me. I forgot I was supposed to be his associate. Not one of the posse. Oops.

"Me? Me?" Jonathan turned to shout at Prudence. "You're the one who believed the aliens were attacking us. You're the one who thought we needed to call NASA. You're the one who believed an extraterrestrial was procreating next door with Mrs. Looper."

"That's only because you made her think that," my mom said. "You wanted to drive Pru crazy."

Jonathan laughed. "Yeah, and if you idiots hadn't gotten involved, I'd have it all now, wouldn't I?"

"All what, Professor?" asked Devon. "What were you after?" Nothing like striking while the iron was hot. An out-of-control suspect was the best kind.

"The gold! What else would anyone want from her?"

Oh, that was low. Very low. So low, I felt like kicking Jonathan myself.

Matilda turned to her friend. "You see, Pru? We told you it was all a setup."

"Let me make sure I have this straight, Steppenhoffer. You married Prudence, then created a world full of aliens to make her believe in them so you could get information about Luckland's alleged gold?"

"Are you a dimwit too?" Jonathan replied, his tone full of snark.

"I like to think I'm fairly intelligent, while you, however, are a complete idiot," Devon answered. "You lied to a police officer here to assist you, and now you've confessed to a crime. I will ask you this only once. Do you wish to press charges against anyone here? Keep in mind there is no statute of limitations on alien hoaxes that may have involved government agencies. All of which is relevant evidence to the current situation."

That was complete mumbo jumbo, and I was so very proud of Devon at that moment.

Our victim, or suspect, still lay on the floor, and he must have realized he was in a bad position because he shook his head.

"You'll have to answer the question verbally, Professor," Devon said.

"No! Okay? I just want to get the hell out of here. You're all nuts."

"Fair enough. We'll release you, and you are free to go wherever you wish, but if you ever step foot in this town again, if you ever contact anyone in this town again, if you ever so much as *breathe* anywhere near this town again, I will hunt you down. Ladies? Go upstairs, and I'll release this subhuman."

My heart did summersaults. That was the Devon I was so fond of. I could have jumped into his arms right then and there, but he shoved me up the stairs. Oh well. There would be time later to thank him—after he apologized.

Once we were all settled in the kitchen with Marcy serving up coffee and scones once again, I turned to Prudence. "How did Jonathan get you to buy into his aliens are invading scheme?"

"I know he's just said he made me think aliens were real, but I know what I saw..."

"What did you see?" I asked.

Prudence shook her head, and Matilda patted Pru's hand. "She thinks she saw aliens in her room, two of them."

"They were staring at her, and one spoke to her. Told her they were coming back, and when they did, they'd invade Earth," Hope said, her tone soft yet angry.

"Then when she told Jonathan, he said she was crazy, that aliens weren't real, even though he'd been the one to introduce her to the idea with all that research into an extraterrestrial's sex life," my mom announced.

"Don't forget about the alien who hitched a ride in my car," Pru declared, color marking her cheeks.

Whether aliens were real or not, Pru certainly believed in them, but she hadn't believed in them while married to Wally or that the statue was an alien when she first saw it. Her belief had come later, *after* she'd become romantically involved with Jonathan. How he'd convinced her was up for debate, and I was sure the women had tried to figure that out over the last thirty years. Maybe I could get Devon to find out from Jonathan. Just then, my phone pinged.

Devon: I'm on my way to Denver with Stepphenhoffer. I'll put him on a bus to Flagstaff.

Me: Is he still taped up?

Devon: He's cuffed. It's fine.

Me: What if he breaks out of them, like Houdini?

Devon: Don't you trust me?

I did trust him, though I was still mad at him. I turned and showed the messages to Matilda. She nodded, then took the phone from me to pass it around. Once they were all satisfied that Devon had things in hand, things settled down.

"Well, I've had enough craziness for a lifetime, or at least a Wednesday in Luckland, so I'm headed for home." Babs stood and leaned over to give Pru a polite squeeze about her shoulders, which was Babs's version of a hug.

I, on the other hand, found myself so intrigued I wanted to stay and learn more, especially about Prudence. There were still too many loose ends I wanted answers to. Why had Pru thought Martin might visit early in the morning? What was the meaning of the strange little box? What happened to Wally, and of course, what was Elroy? Plus, with Devon out of town for a little while on his errand, someone had to keep the ladies out of trouble. If that were even possible.

CHAPTER TWENTY-FOUR

"Pru, can I ask a question?"

"Of course, Pippa, dear, anything."

"Why did you think it might be Martin at the door this morning?"

"Well, Martin is an old friend, Pip," Prudence replied with a wistful sigh. "You know we were a thing back in high school."

From his reaction when she disappeared, I suspected something was between them. "But that doesn't really explain about now. I mean, it's been nearly fifty years."

"Not quite that long, Pip, but I see your point. I suppose you could say our timing has never been particularly good. It's rather a long story. Shall I sum it up?"

"Actually, I'd love the full details, if you don't mind." Having the entire story would explain a whole lot. Not just about Prudence, but all the ladies. "How about we sit on the sofa, and you can fill me in."

Naturally, everyone came with us. There really wasn't any such thing as a private conversation in this town. At least the conversation would be about Prudence and not me. I sat on the couch with Prudence on my right, my mom on my left, Matilda in the recliner, and Hope and Marcy on the loveseat. Matilda reached over and handed Prudence what appeared to be a yearbook. I wondered where it came from. My mother had never shown that one to me. Prudence opened it to the homecoming page, with a picture of Martin and Prudence. King and Queen.

I let out a whistle. "You two were one hot couple, Pru. I mean seriously hot."

They were also so young and completely opposite to Devon and my yearbook photos. We weren't homecoming material back then. Not like Martin and Prudence. Prudence wore a sparkly disco dress, and Martin had decked out in a white, wide-lapel tux.

Prudence sighed next to me. "He was something, wasn't he? I wasn't bad either."

I glanced at her and suddenly saw her as the young and vulnerable girl in the photo. I had an immediate urge to photograph her at that moment, to let her see herself for who she still was.

"He asked me out the first time on the playground at recess in second grade," she said.

If my heart wasn't already mush, that would do it.

"He asked if I'd play hide and seek with him, so I pushed him down and ran away." She laughed. Not the drunken cackle I was used to from Pru. A pure girlish laugh. Almost a giggle. "First day of junior high, he tried to sit next to me at lunch. He brought me an oatmeal snack cake. I took the cake and all my stuff and went to a different table."

I started to feel sorry for the guy.

"Then the next year, there was a Sadie Hawkins dance. You know where girls ask boys."

"You asked him?" I was really excited now. This was a good story.

"Don't be silly. I couldn't let Martin know I liked him. Even if I did. I asked his best friend."

"Oh my god, you went with his best friend?" I felt a little mad at her for that.

"No. Martin was seriously angry, and they ended up in a fistfight. They both got grounded, and I had no date at all. I felt really bad, so I baked some brownies and took them to Martin's house, where we watched TV, and he put his arm around me. Then he kissed me. That was it. We were together after that until I went to college."

"And then?" I asked, practically on the edge of my seat.

"Being apart is hard, Pippa. He drifted. I drifted. Who knows? Eventually, I met Wally, and you know the rest."

Did I? I sensed way more.

"Let's have lunch, ladies," my mom said quite abruptly. "It's been an exhausting few days. Pippa, why don't you set the table outside? Hope and Marcy will throw something together, and Tillie and I will unload the rest of the things from the RV."

We left Prudence flipping through her yearbook as I scrounged up some table settings. Pru's story really had me thinking though. Martin and Pru were almost star-crossed. Together as kids, growing up with each other, going from dislike to like, to so much more, then drifting apart. It was a bit like Devon and me. Hearing Pru tell her tale, I felt as if I suddenly understood how easy it was to become careless. To waste such an incredible gift. Pru and Martin needed to be together again and become an honest-to-goodness second chance love story.

Considering the last few days had been brutal in terms of surprises, lunch was remarkably uneventful. I figured I'd head home, grab my little silver box, then pop over to the shop and finish working on the new shipment. First, I wanted to ask Pru one more question. I waited for everyone to begin clearing up the lunch remains, leaving just Prudence and me at the table, then I got up my nerve.

"Say, Pru, will you tell me about Teddy?"

She sighed somewhat ruefully. "Another mistake, Pip. Just another mistake."

Pru didn't know Devon and I had seen the photos of her with Teddy, but there was no need to divulge that. She could just tell her story in her own way.

"Go on," I said.

"I'd just returned to Luckland, you know, after the fiasco with Jonathan, and I discovered the ladies had kept a terrible secret from me. Martin had married."

"You hadn't seen that coming, had you?"

"No, and it broke my heart. So, I went to a matchmaker."

I blinked. "You had a matchmaker here in Luckland?" That was news.

"Oh, no, in Denver. You can find anything in Denver," she said with a grin. Then just like that, the grin disappeared. "But I don't recommend it at all. It didn't turn out well for me."

"Teddy's death wasn't your fault. You said Jonathan caused Teddy's death, right?" I hoped she was over Teddy. I didn't want to dredge up bad memories.

"Well, yes, but Teddy was no prize, believe me. I didn't know Jonathan was after the gold, but Teddy definitely was. He would ask me about it over and over."

"Gold? You mean Luckland's gold?" I shook my head. I couldn't believe how many people thought it existed and would go to such lengths to find it.

"Of course. Do you remember when Babs first met Tom?"

I did. Babs brought him to dinner, and the ladies grilled him for hours. I didn't understand the questions back then. I just figured it was the ladies' usual maternal meddling. It seemed there was more to it.

"I do remember. You put him through the wringer."

"We had to. We had to make sure his intentions were pure. That he wasn't marrying Babs because of the gold."

"I know the legend of the gold keeps this town humming, Pru, but seriously, is there any, and do any of you know where it is?"

She looked up then, past my shoulder, so I followed her gaze.

CHAPTER TWENTY-FIVE

"Am I interrupting?" Devon asked.

I could have said yes, but not when he looked so handsome as he leaned against the doorway, tipping his head in that way he did.

"Not at all, we're just finishing up," I said with what I hoped was a natural smile, even though I'd already mentally ticked off ways I could get together discreetly with Pru and finish the conversation.

"Hang on a moment, Pip," Prudence said suddenly. "Did you say Dani is coming home and bringing her new guy?"

"I did. Why?"

"Then perhaps, Devon, you ought to sit down," she said. Then, much louder, she yelled for my mom. "Kate, bring the girls out here."

The girls. I supposed I'd still be calling Dani a girl when we were old too.

Several minutes later, the *girls* all filed out to the patio. Marcy carried a tray of beverages and joined us. I wondered what on earth Pru wanted to tell us and what it had to do with Dani.

"As soon as Babs gets here, we'll get started," said my mom. I didn't realize Babs was needed, and I became a tad concerned.

Devon sat next to me, then, for whatever reason, took hold of my hand. I admit it gave me goose bumps. He was sucking up or perhaps just gauging my mood. I stole a peek at him, and he gave me one of his winks and a grin. I internally groaned. Staying mad at him was going to be difficult. Really, really difficult. Climbing Mt. Everest difficult. In winter. In shorts.

"Okay, now we're all here, let's get to it," said Pru with an odd amount of authority as Babs stepped outside and joined us. "Dani is coming home and bringing her new beau. It's up to all of us to make sure he's suitable."

Damn it. Whatever the ladies had planned, it would not be good.

"I'm sure he's very nice," I said, though I had no idea if he was or wasn't. Dani had told me a bit about him, and she'd sent a few pics. He was attractive, I supposed, in a pompous sort of way, but if Dani liked him, he must have had a redeeming quality or two.

My mother looked at me. "He probably *is* very nice, Pip, but we have to be careful. Now, tell us what you know."

"Me?" I hadn't realized I was supposed to be some sort of stool pigeon. Devon squeezed my hand for support. By now, he knew all the signs that I was getting uncomfortable.

"Easy, Red," he said, his voice pitched low and calming. "You're not ratting her out for murder here."

Okay, point taken, but Dani was my best friend. I had never betrayed her confidence and was wholly ill at ease in doing so, even if it was for her benefit.

"I don't know much," I said. "His name is Jake Burns. He's a shipwreck explorer, I suppose. He has a boat and goes out looking for sunken treasure or some such thing. Dani was part of his last dive crew in the South Pacific. She told me about him when she was home last month. Guess they hit it off. Really, that's all I know."

Then the ladies began firing off questions, none of them waiting for answers. Typical.

"How old is he?" asked Matilda.

"Where is he from?" asked my mom.

"Is he wealthy?" asked Prudence.

"How did she get the job?" asked Hope.

Devon held up a hand to stop the assault. "One at a time, ladies," he said, chuckling. It worked. That was a first.

"Pippa?" He smiled as a prompt for me to continue.

"From the photo I saw, I'm guessing he's around forty. He's from Newport, Rhode Island Old money, supposedly. How she got the job, no clue. Probably the usual, someone contacted her to join their dive crew."

"When do they arrive?" my mom asked.

"Friday, and before you ask, I'm not sure what time."

"Good. We'll have plenty of time to get Rosa up here." My mom began typing into her phone.

"What? Why are you bringing Dani's mother up here?" I didn't quite shout, but not only was I surprised, having my mother calling Dani's mother would not sit well with Dani. As far as I knew, Rosa hadn't come back to visit since they'd moved down to Tucson a few years back. Not that Dani wouldn't want to see her mom, but maybe she wasn't ready for the big introduction yet. Having me meet Jake was one thing, but the entire posse? Including her mother? I didn't think that was a spectacular idea at all.

"Because this involves her just as much as the rest of us," she replied.

Babs looked utterly confused, as I was. Devon, suspiciously, did not.

"Say there, Yoda, what do you know?" I asked him. "You do not look surprised at this."

"That's because, my young Jedi, nothing surprises me anymore. I am the police chief; it is my business not to be surprised."

I narrowed my gaze, giving him my most pointed look, hopefully expressing my displeasure at his flippancy. He just shrugged.

"Somebody needs to explain all this, please," said Babs, her voice resigned. "I do have to get back home and relieve Tom of his Leah-sitting responsibilities. As fascinating as this is, of course."

I was sure she added that last bit for good measure. Sometimes, she could be as snarky as me. That was the twin thing.

"Yes, yes, Babs, we're getting to that," said Pru.

Pru turned to Hope. "Maybe you should explain it to them."

Hope cleared her throat. She liked to do that. It was the librarian in her. "As you all know, Dani's father, Pedro, came here from the Dominican Republic to play ball. He had a wicked arm, as they say, and played for the Rockies. Rosa technically came from Florida, but her mother was Cuban, which is why Dani is such a stunner. She got her physical fitness from her dad and her incredible beauty from Rosa."

"Hope, no offense, but where are you going with this?" I asked, unable to not voice my impatience.

Hope smiled, not taking offense at all. "When Pedro came to play in Denver, they settled here in Luckland. Trivial and ordinary enough on the surface, but their landing in Luckland was no accident."

"You know my grandmother, Eleanor, had a younger brother," said Prudence, adding to the story, which I didn't think helped.

"Yes, that's right," said Hope. "Sean O'Connor, Jr."

I looked at Babs to see if that made it all clear. Nope.

"Now, Sean liked to travel, and during his younger days was quite adventurous. One summer, he landed in Cuba. That was where he met Esmerelda. It was the mid-thirties you know, and Havana was becoming quite the hot spot. They called it the Paris of the Caribbean."

That was why Hope was telling the story. She had a head full of history to impart. Today's history lesson was quite intriguing, though, and I leaned forward.

"Sean and Esmerelda fell in love, and even though neither was fluently bilingual, they managed to communicate. Sean decided to settle there, and they married. This was before the revolution, of course. Sean and Esmerelda had a daughter, Elena. It was Elena and her husband who fled to Miami after the revolution. That was where Rosa was born and raised."

"Wait. Rosa is Sean O'Connor's granddaughter, and Sean is Prudence's great-uncle. That means she's Pru's cousin!" Babs was actually following along. I was impressed.

"That's right," said Prudence. "I suppose we've never had a reason to mention it, but we're second cousins."

"That's why you feel it's necessary to grill Dani's new boyfriend? Seems a bit over the top, don't you think? Having a family tree seminar?" That earned me another hand squeeze. Okay, maybe I was a little derisive.

"Really, Pip, don't be silly," said my mom. "There's something very serious behind all this. Dani is a true Lucklander, and as such, she's vulnerable to charlatans and gold diggers."

"What if this Jake fellow is after the gold, Pippa?" asked Matilda. "He's a treasure hunter who happens to meet a young woman from Luckland, home of the legendary gold. After what you've witnessed with Pru's ex this morning, you realize we have to know for sure."

"You certainly don't want Dani to be played as I was, Pip," said Pru.

"Perhaps you don't recognize the danger because you've got Devon," said Hope. "You don't have to worry about it."

I looked at Devon then, who stared at me with a very strange expression. I couldn't read it too well. I felt as if he were asking me something. I just wasn't sure what.

"They did it to Tom, Pip, so we're also gonna have to let them do it to Jake," said Babs. I think she felt vindicated. Or vengeful.

What I didn't understand was why being a true Lucklander made us specifically vulnerable to gold diggers. It wasn't as if being a descendant from one of the founders meant we had any information on the gold they never found. Unless they had found gold, and we, or rather, the posse, did have information —a secret they refused to share. A secret I had a feeling they had hidden in those shoeboxes. Devon was right. I really needed to talk to him, but in order to do that, I needed to get this meeting adjourned, and quickly.

"Why don't we just have Devon investigate him, hmm? Seems that's a far easier solution?"

Devon smiled at me. "You know, I think that's a superb idea. I can find out more about him, which might reveal his intentions. If his background check works out, Dani and Jake can go down and meet her family in Tucson."

"I vote we let Mr. Clean do the honors," I said. "All in favor, say aye." Then I waited. Nobody said aye. "Come on, ladies."

One by one, I got a positive response—hesitant but audible.

Devon stood up, tugging on my hand as he did so. I assumed he wanted me to get up and tag along with him. Maybe he was ready to apologize. He walked me to my Jeep, then opened the door for me to get in.

"Can I come home?" he asked.

"Home?"

"Yeah," he whispered. "Home."

While his request to come home was a very significant step forward, it wasn't an apology. Still, I missed him. Normally, not being with him all the time wouldn't faze me, but because we'd been quarreling, twenty-four hours seemed to stretch longer than a single day. Being without him hurt—a horrible hurt in my heart only he could cause.

I did what anyone in my shoes would do. I nodded. With a smile, he closed the door, and I drove off.

CHAPTER TWENTY-SIX

With the sky darkening over the horizon, 99 and I had just begun to relax on the back porch when the crunch of tires sounded in the driveway. Devon, I assumed, even though it had been hours since I got home. He must have taken one hell of a detour from my mom's house.

I lifted 99 into my arms, then trekked inside. In an impromptu move to pretend I hadn't been waiting for him, I nabbed a book I'd been off and on reading and plopped into the recliner before he came in. The minute the front door opened, I flipped open the book to a random page and stared at it. A few minutes later, after the rustle of him placing items on the kitchen counter, his footsteps signaled his entry into the family room. I feigned total absorption in my book.

"Good book?" he asked.

"Fabulous."

"Would it be more fabulous if I turned on a light and you could actually see what you're reading?"

"I'm practicing for winter blackouts, so no, thank you." When my stubbornness set in, there was no stopping it.

"I see. Well, carry on. I'll fix something for us to eat, but I might need a light or two if that won't disturb you."

"No, Kemosabe, you may carry on." I waved him off. At that point, I was being ridiculous. He knew it too, but that was the thing—he let me be me. Several minutes passed, with him making various prepping noises in the kitchen. Then he stood in front of me with a glass of wine.

"*Pour moi?*" He preferred beer, so the wine clearly was for me.

"But of course." He smiled, handed it to me, then retreated to the kitchen. I could have just gone over there and assisted. I could have, but I sensed his actions were a part of his apology— because he still needed to make one.

The kitchen and family room shared the same floor space, so as I wasn't actually reading the book, I stole glances and spied on him. He was quite the handy kitchen guy. He chopped, he diced, he set a beautiful table, and he could cook. He'd just put whatever he'd made in the oven before he came over to claim the sofa. He barely fit on it if he lay down. He had to put his feet over one armrest and his head on the other. He folded his hands behind his head to prop it higher and looked over at me.

"Am I forgiven?" he asked, raising one eyebrow, a half-smile playing on his lips.

"Are you apologizing?"

"I might be, though it depends on what I'm apologizing for."

"For implying I was a member of the ladies' posse and trying to control you and run your life. You have to know I would never try to control you, and I'm nothing like those women. Nothing."

"I do know, and you're right, I shouldn't have said that."

"Is that your apology? Because if it is, it's lacking."

Devon smiled. "Maybe if you came over here and sat by me, I could think about how to increase it some more."

Going over there was a mistake, but the magnetic forcefield that was Devon just sucked me over, and once there, all bets were off. We had a few minutes to kill while whatever he'd put in the oven finished, so we made fairly good use of those minutes with more than a few steamy kisses. We were only human, after all.

When the oven buzzer went off, I turned to look at him and had to smile. A lock of golden-brown hair hung carelessly in front of one eye, and stubble lined his jaw. To me, he was ruggedly handsome, especially with his amazing greenish-blue eyes. I wanted to stay and cuddle for a little longer. Hunger, though, had me getting up and heading for the kitchen, Devon right behind me.

"Go sit," he said. "I'll get it."

I sighed, deciding right then and there that everyone should have a Devon. Just not my particular Devon.

I sat and played queen of the castle while he served up a beautiful salad and a baked rotini-style pasta with roasted veggies in garlic sauce.

"I assumed you took some time to make sure Steppenhoffer got to Flagstaff, and that was why you didn't follow me home right away."

Devon sighed. "Yes. When I put the professor on the bus back to Arizona, I told him we'd be keeping an eye on him. So, I had to arrange for someone to follow the professor from the bus in Flagstaff and to let him know we meant business."

"You can do that? And who might *we* be?"

"Yes, and I still have friends in the bureau."

"Well, I'm glad that's taken care of, and before I forget, I should mention that I researched the little silver box. Steppenhoffer bought it from the IUAS. I checked with Belle. What's interesting is I can't find out how the shop acquired it. There's no paper trail. It just...appeared."

"Yeah, that is interesting, but honestly, I'm not surprised. There has been some really weird stuff going on recently, like our little friend Elroy. He wasn't made of anything extraterrestrial, but he was unusual. Elroy was a composite of concrete, glass, and plaster. Almost like a ceramic with a very hot glaze, which gave it a metallic sheen. Remember when it broke, it shattered, like glass."

"What about his sibling?"

"Same thing. Jonathan Steppenhoffer was, *is*, a trifle mad, you know. I sense he bought all these things to frighten Prudence and make her believe there were aliens among us—which she still does."

"I don't suppose you asked him how or why he blew up the basement or even how he managed to convince Pru that aliens were real?"

"Well, we don't know he had anything to do with the basement. It still might be related to the shoeboxes and whoever had them."

I shook my head. "You thought that. I think it has to do with Jonathan."

"Okay, I agree, and yes, I did ask. He denied any involvement, and regarding Pru... He just kept repeating the woman was crazy. I got so angry I wanted to punch him. Instead, I'm getting a full background check done on him. Hopefully, that will lead us to something we can convict him on. Right now, I can't do anything more."

I nodded, though I didn't like it. "What about the vial?"

"The lab is still testing it."

"So, we're at an impasse."

"Maybe not. What about Teddy? Did you learn anything more about him from Pru?"

"A bit, but you came in right at the moment she was telling all, you know."

"Sorry!" He grinned. He was so not sorry.

"Well, it seems Teddy was the result of a matchmaker. He was also after Luckland's 'gold.' Are there any men in Colorado not looking for the gold? Other than you, of course."

"Do you think there is any gold? I mean, McConnell seemed to think there was, and he's a descendant of a founder. Jonathan obviously believed him. Maybe there's some truth to the rumors."

I stared at him. Devon was not one to indulge in rumors, but I'd been thinking along the same lines. "Have you ever taken a look at the map the founders used to get to Luckland?"

"Not really. I know it's a star navigational map, but that's all."

"Exactly. And how would anyone find gold using that? Wouldn't a topographical map be more effective in showing someone where there was gold?"

Devon smiled. "Yes, but they weren't widely used until the mid-1850s. Most frontier settlers relied on the stars to help pinpoint their location and areas of uncharted land. So, whoever our founders bought the map from maybe only had a star navigational map to approximate where Luckland now stands today. For all we know, the gold could be ten or twenty miles from here, forever hidden at the bottom of a valley."

"True. Or, the founders found the gold, and the information about its location is in those shoeboxes."

I waited for Devon's reaction. He grinned. "I like the way your mind works, Pip. I know we still need to find those boxes, though I'm not sure how. In the meantime, I don't think it will hurt if we find as much information as possible about the map the founders used, where it came from, and where exactly it led."

I smiled in agreement, then remembered something. "The professor and the Panellos." I couldn't believe I hadn't associated the two before. "When the Panellos held us hostage, they said they'd still be looking for the women and the Vegas money if they hadn't run into a professor. Prudence and the others were stunned when Frankie mentioned a professor. Do you think the Panellos meant Professor Steppenhoffer? Had they run into him somewhere, and he mentioned Prudence?"

"That's quite far-fetched—"

"But not out of the realms of possibility."

"Well, it's a huge coincidence."

"And you don't like coincidences, I know. Still, it's a thought." I could always ask the women if they knew any other professors. "So, we find out information on the founders' map. I wonder if it has anything to do with the map Pru bought. Did you ask her about it?"

"Actually, yes. I meant to tell you. She said she was writing a paper in Jonathan's class on star maps—something she was interested in because of Luckland's map. He suggested the IUAS catalog, of which he had a copy, and she bought the map."

"That's it?"

"Yep."

"So, nothing odd or suspicious about it? Nothing revelational?"

"Not according to Pru."

"Hmm."

"I know that look in your eye, Pippa. I think we can put that particular mystery to bed."

"Talking about bed..."

Devon grinned again, but before I pushed away from the table, I needed one more piece of information. "Have you done anything about Jake? They'll be here Friday."

"Already on it. They're staying here?" A tiny frown marred Devon's brow

"Yes, Devon. Dani always stays here. They won't be in the way." I tried to sound confident, but my house wasn't that big. We'd make do though. "What do you mean you're on it? How so?"

"I'm making inquiries, and I'll keep you posted. I promise."

That was where our conflict arose. I had a very great need to know everything, and he tended to be secretive—which I suspected would never change.

CHAPTER TWENTY-SEVEN

DEVON: DON'T MAKE PLANS FOR D. TOLD M&P WE'D MEET UP AT café.

I glared at my phone for two reasons. First, texting shorthand wasn't my thing. I had to concentrate to decipher. *Plans for D.* Dinner. Easy enough. Don't make plans for dinner. *M&P?* I had no clue. The second reason was that I'd spent all morning cleaning the house. Housekeeping wasn't my thing, but as Dani was due tomorrow, I made an effort. Needless to say, after a thorough scrubbing and dusting, I was ready for a nice long nap.

With a sigh, I dragged my butt upstairs to shower. What I should have done was select something to wear first. I had a terrible habit of getting out of the shower and wandering through my closet, looking for exactly the right outfit while dripping wet.

Thursday night at the café. Casual, yes, but as I'd be with Devon, not totally casual because I had to look good. Alluring. Irresistible. That was the thing about being imperfect—as most humans were—we had to have some extraordinary qualities to make up for our flaws. I certainly had a few.

In the end, I went with simple jeans and a peasant blouse. I left my hair down because Devon had a thing for long, curly red tresses, and I added some flashy earrings and a coral lipstick guaranteed to stay on even in an intense lip-lock—something I intended to have.

I was ready to head downstairs when Devon came home. I smiled because having Devon here was the best thing that had happened to me all day, which made me realize how deeply I was all in. Of course, with my little bullhorn episode in the RV, he knew exactly where I stood. I would have liked to know if he was all in too. Though positive he was, he hadn't said anything, and I would have loved to hear the words.

I headed down just as he headed up. We met about halfway, and he greeted me the way I hoped he always would.

"Well, hello to you too," I said when we came up for air.

"Back at ya. I'll be down in a jiff, and we'll head over, okay?"

"Okay, but first, who exactly are we meeting for dinner?" I asked, wanting a heads up.

"You're not very good with ciphers, are you? No worries, you'll learn." He smiled, took the remaining steps two at a time, and left me hanging.

We'd barely walked through the café door when a waving Prudence caught my eye.

"Yoohoo! Pippa, Devon, this way."

She sat at a table with Martin. M and P. I should have known. I looked up at Devon, who had the silliest grin as if he knew the reaction he'd get. So, I elbowed him, sure he'd expect it. Sometimes, the two of us were just our eight-year-old selves in adult bodies. Granted, being unable to figure out who M&P were was rather funny, so I also grinned.

I sat down in the chair Devon politely pulled out for me. I did wonder, for just a second, if he was going to pull it out from under me the same way he had when we were at seventh-grade assembly. That stayed with me no matter how hard I tried to let go. My butt hurt for days after that, and it wasn't any consolation to learn boys did those things because they liked you.

"Well, Deputy, you are certainly looking quite dashing tonight," I said, safely in my seat. Martin did look snazzy in jeans and a flannel shirt, with his neat, thick salt and pepper hair visible without his deputy hat. He kind of had an old-west vibe. Pretty hot, really—for an older guy.

"How about you just call me Martin, Pippa," he replied with a smile and a wink. That earned him an elbow from Prudence. The spark of familiarity between them showed they'd known each other their whole lives, and that connection was still there.

Because they were working, Marcy and Hope came over to say hello and take our order for drinks and appetizers, including my favorite of bison short rib sliders. With their amazing signature sauce, they were to die for. The first time I'd tried them, I had suggested they consider selling them to some Denver bars for late-night snackers. I even did a photo shoot to help market the dish, but with all the mayhem lately, with someone leaking their cheesecake and lasagna recipes online, they'd put the whole project aside.

We sat back and chatted for a while, though I wanted to learn more about Prudence and Martin's relationship. The way they looked at each other, and the way he smiled at her... Martin and Prudence together were just joyful. However, I did wonder why they hadn't reconnected sooner, given that Martin had been a widower for at least twenty years. Something had to have been in the way, and I wanted to know what that was. So, I did what any nosy person would do. I asked.

"I don't mean to pry, well, yes, I do, but why have you two waited so long to do this? You know, go out, on a date, with each other?" I hoped I wasn't embarrassing them, but understanding their dynamics felt important.

"We were hurt and angry, Pippa. Worst of all, we held on to our anger. Sometimes, and I'm sure you know this, we use anger to mask grief. We broke each other's hearts, and we didn't know how to fix it," Prudence said.

"That's right." Martin placed his hand over Pru's and gently squeezed. "Instead of blaming ourselves for drifting apart and not keeping in touch, we blamed each other. We wasted a lot of years that way. I had no idea she was going through hell."

Prudence smiled—a beautiful happy smile. "I had no idea he still cared. However, we certainly aren't going to waste any more time. We have catching up to do!"

I looked at Devon to see if he understood, as I did, what they were saying, but his expression was hard to read. Before I could ask him what was wrong, our drinks and appetizers arrived.

"So, Pip, have you heard from Dani?" Prudence asked. "We're all anxious to see her."

"You mean you're anxious to interrogate the new guy."

Devon glanced at me. "Hopefully, there won't be a need. I anticipate a full report by morning, which will tell us a lot about the man."

Be that as it may, the report wouldn't tell us everything, and I doubted we'd know for certain who Jake was until he and Devon were face to face. In reality, I was counting on Devon and Matilda's intuitive powers to ensure Jake was on the up and up.

"Yes, dear, of course, but we'll still need to make up our own minds. You understand," said Prudence. "We will not allow Dani or Pippa"—she paused for emphasis—"to ever experience the kind of pain I did. We are clear on that, right?"

Wow. That was a clear warning to Devon that when push

came to shove, they would put me above him in our relationship. I wasn't sure that was fair, but I did appreciate their support.

"Devon, pay them no mind," Martin said. "The women in this town tend to stick together. It's not a reflection on you, trust me. I would know." He grinned.

I held back a sigh. They were quite a couple, and I felt like the Grinch must have as his heart grew.

"Don't worry, Prudence. Pippa is the one person in this world I'd never hurt. Well, except my mom. I wouldn't hurt her either. Or you or Kate or Hope or Marcy," Devon said.

I laughed and shook my head. "You were doing so well, Kemosabe."

"Well, now. Hello there. Has everyone decided what they're going to have for their main course?" Morgan asked as she sidled up to our table.

Leave it to the town flirt to spoil my mood. Devon and I grew up with her. She was single and liked to peddle her wares, as Matilda liked to say. Morgan also, unfortunately, worked part-time at the café and seemed to be our server for the evening.

"Devon. Or is it Chief now?" she coyly asked as she placed a hand on his shoulder. As if that was necessary. "What can I get you? I'm going to recommend the trout. Having to stay in shape the way you do. You must work out daily, I imagine." She trailed her hand down to his biceps.

I was ready to knock her flat because I was really getting fed up with her not keeping her hands off him when she knew he was taken, but I waited to see what he'd do.

"You know, Morgan, I'm going to go with the pot pie," Devon said with a grin. "Pippa here likes a little meat on my bones if you know what I mean."

He winked at me. I didn't know which made me happier, his

answer or the look on her face. Priceless. Morgan stalked off, which was good riddance as far as I was concerned. I just hoped she didn't plan on putting arsenic in my food.

"Well done, Devon," said Prudence, her voice lowered. "You're coming along nicely."

"Thank you, Prudence." He smiled at me. "Pip, you can thank me later."

"Perhaps I will. Perhaps." I said that last *perhaps* to keep him on his toes, but I couldn't help the little warmth that bubbled inside my chest at the way he'd given me a chance to witness and understand Prudence and Martin's relationship in all its complexity. Devon wanted me to see what *we* could have together. I fell just a little deeper in love with him right at that moment.

CHAPTER TWENTY-EIGHT

Devon had stolen the recliner, so I was just getting comfy on the couch when he sat up suddenly—eyes sharp and focused, staring down at his phone.

"What is it," I asked.

"Jake Burns. AKA Jacob Wallingford. AKA, are you ready for this?" Devon glanced up. "Jacob Steppenhoffer."

"Shut the front door!" I hopped off the couch and went to sit on the arm of the recliner. "How? Who? I need more."

"We both do. This is astonishing."

"What else is there?"

"How about we open that laptop of yours? I feel we need to do a bit of research. Call it a hunch."

We headed to the kitchen table, where I fired up Roadrunner. Then Devon forwarded the report so we could pull it up on the screen.

I stared at the information but couldn't make much sense of all the abbreviations. "What's that mean?" I asked, but before he could answer, I pointed to the next item. "What about that?"

Devon took my hand, then placed it on the table under his own and held it there.

"How about you give me a minute or two to tell you what we've got? Then I'll decipher all the codes for you. Deal?"

I didn't have much choice, so I sighed and agreed.

"Okay. So, here's what we have. Jacob Steppenhoffer, born 1980, Roswell, New Mexico." He clicked on a link, and up popped a photo. In it were Winston, Belle, Jonathan, and another woman. Identified as Pearlanne Smythe. Opening a new tab, we searched Pearlanne and found an obituary. She died in eighty-nine in a car accident, but prior to that, she worked at the IUAS in Roswell as an assistant to Winston McConnell II.

I was dumbstruck, to be honest. It appeared Devon was too. We stared at the screen for a moment. Then at each other. Then back at the screen. "We're going to have to call Belle, aren't we?"

"It appears so." Devon almost sighed at that, as if it were all too much.

"I'll get the wine."

"Do you think that's enough? Perhaps we ought to break out something more potent. Like that cheesecake in the fridge." Leave it to Devon to make a joke at a time like this.

I got the wine and cheesecake, and we settled back at the table, ready for what might be an awfully uncomfortable conversation. He placed his phone on the table and dialed Belle with the speaker on. I glanced at him to see if I could read his mood, but he had on his investigative mask. Stone-faced, I called it. I poured him a glass of wine and sliced him an extra-large piece of cake.

The phone rang a few times before she answered.

"Belle Chantelle." She spoke quickly as if in a hurry.

"Belle. Devon and Pippa here. How are you?"

"Fine, fine, just on my way out. What can I do for you? I've put all the ledgers away, I'm afraid, so if you need a lookup, it may have to wait."

"No worries on that front, Belle, but there is one thing. Do you recall a woman named Pearlanne Smythe?"

Silence.

"We're only asking because my oldest and dearest friend has a new…someone in her life, and there's something odd about him. He's a treasure hunter by the name of Jake Burns. We think he was born in Roswell to this Pearlanne Smythe, who may have worked for you. Does that ring a bell?" I swore I heard her sigh with relief.

"Can't say I know the fellow," she replied, completely avoiding the question about his mother.

"He also uses the name Wallingford. Jacob Wallingford," Devon said.

Silence again. Uh-oh. She should have just said no right away because she'd now raised my suspicions.

"Belle?" I tried to sound concerned as if we'd lost her.

"Yes, I'm here. Wallingford. Well, now. This friend of yours, is she from Luckland?"

"Dani. Yes, in fact, she's, as you say, one of us."

"Oh dear. Oh, my stars. Well," Belle said, exhaling loudly.

"Belle, is everything all right?" Devon asked.

"I suppose it was going to come out somehow someday. Pearlanne worked for us, yes. Sweet thing, but she made the terrible mistake of… What is it you say now, hooking up? With Jonathan Steppenhoffer. She was young and innocent, but nine months later, she had a son. The Wallingfords adopted him. The professor didn't want anything to do with her or the baby. Bit of a scurvy scoundrel if you ask me."

"Quite right," said Devon. "Are the Wallingfords still in Roswell?"

"Oh, no, they moved to Florida years ago when Jacob, if that's what they called him, was still in diapers, I think. Pearlanne was heartbroken, but open adoptions weren't a thing then. Unfortunately, she didn't live long enough to see him again. Tragic what happened. Car accident, you know."

"That *is* quite tragic. Well, thank you for clarifying all that. Take care now," I said before disconnecting. With our info confirmed, we now had a dilemma on our hands.

"This isn't looking good," I said to Devon. "Dani deserves better than a fraud."

"We don't know if he's a fraud just yet. They'll be here tomorrow. We have to act as if we know nothing, and under no circumstances do we inform the posse. None. Deal?" He held out his hand and gave me the stare down. "Pip?" Brows raised, he cocked his head and waited.

"Deal, but I'm not going to like it," I said, shaking his hand.

"Oh yes, you will. I promise you that." He pulled me up from the chair and sealed the deal with those patent-pending lips.

Knowing Dani was on the way, I was so excited I barely slept. I was also incredibly nervous knowing the bad news Devon and I would have to share.

By the time the sun rose, I'd already detected the delicious scent of bacon wafting up the stairs. I wondered if Devon had also made waffles. I did love waffles, though I also loved his French toast, which was also pretty awesome, especially with fresh peaches. Then I remembered we hadn't hit the farmers market lately, and most likely, we'd be having omelets.

Somehow, he'd managed not just the French toast and bacon but also scrambled eggs. The coffee also smelled heavenly, which, together with Devon's smile, put me in a calmer mood. He handed me my mug before plating the food and carrying it to the table.

We sat in companionable silence until Devon got up to leave.

I cleared my throat before he got too far. "Aren't you forgetting something?"

He grinned and leaned down to give me a kiss. "For luck," he said, then started whistling on his way out the door.

Why I needed luck, I wasn't sure. Unless it was to clean the mess he'd left behind in the kitchen. The man was a brilliant cook, but the dirty pots and pans he left behind were legendary.

Not five minutes later, I got a text.

Dani: Just landed! See you soon.

I did a half-assed job with the dishes, hoping the high-end dishwasher would do its thing. Then I tried to vacuum all the remnants 99 had left. She shed a lot—big balls of white fluff that seemed to be everywhere. Once I'd finished cleaning, I had just enough time to shower and change. I couldn't wait to see Dani and have some quality girl time, but until Devon and I unearthed more about Jake, I also needed to keep Dani unaware of what we'd learned. I wasn't about to destroy her relationship until we had all the facts.

When the doorbell rang, I was ready. At least, I hoped I was. I opened the door, expecting to have our usual greeting, one we'd invented as kids. So, it took me aback when she simply stood there next to Jake and looked at him as if waiting for him to...give her permission to say hello? I frowned. Dani and I should have been hugging and doing a little dance. Instead, I waved them in as if they were strangers.

"Please, come in." I didn't recognize my voice. We went into the living room, and after we'd sat, I smiled in an attempt to bring things back to normal. "Where's your luggage?"

"We'll be staying at the Inn, Pippa. Jake thought we'd be more comfortable. Didn't you, honey?"

If I thought my voice sounded odd, Dani's was downright bizarre. I had to get Devon home. Dani was suddenly a Stepford wife. We'd been friends for almost twenty-five years. This was not Dani. She trained Navy SEALs and dove for sunken treasure. The woman was a force to be reckoned with—not someone who should be playing the submissive to this oaf. He wasn't even all that good-looking. Not that it mattered, but since he didn't seem to have any other redeeming qualities like a great personality, or *any* personality, I didn't see the attraction. The pictures she'd sent made him look somehow more debonair with a seafaring captain appearance. Sitting on my sofa, with thinning hair streaked with gray and a somewhat pointy face, he looked...harsh.

"How about I get us some coffee." I stood, and Dani started to get up with me. Jake shook his head and put his hand on her arm. She meekly sat back down. Horrified, I headed into the kitchen. They could still see me from the sofa, but desperate to text Devon, I hid my phone under the counter.

Me: They're here. Need you to come. Now.

Devon: I should be home by lunch.

Me: NOW. Emergency.

It was hard to convey a complex situation in a text, so I certainly hoped he understood.

Devon: On my way.

He added a heart emoji. I smiled at that but was more grateful he'd be here in around five minutes. It would take me that long to get the coffee going, but even if it didn't, I decided to wait for him to arrive before I went back to the living room. I was really creeped out because Dani should be in the kitchen with me, helping me while we gossiped and giggled, not sitting stiffly on the sofa next to a goon like that. Jake had done something to her, I was sure, and I had to hope Devon could fix whatever it was.

CHAPTER TWENTY-NINE

I waited until the security chime on the front door warned me Devon had arrived, then I picked up the coffee tray and carried it out to meet him in the living room. Neither Dani nor Jake stood to say hello to him, which was even more creepy. Devon nodded a greeting.

"Dani, good to see you," he said quite formally. It was his police voice. Oh, dear.

"Jake Burns," Jake said with a nod. Though I had no idea why, he looked and sounded smug, and I wanted to wipe that look off his face.

"Jake, nice to meet you, and please don't get up." Devon's response held a little snark, and I suppressed a grin.

I set down the tray, then sat on the loveseat, patting the cushion for Devon to sit as well. The second he gave me a slight head shake, I realized Devon had learned something new between when I texted, and he arrived. Whatever he'd found wasn't good, and I had a horrible feeling Devon would arrest Jake. Or beat the crap out of him.

I was just about to ask Dani about their flight, anything to break the awkward silence, when a knock sounded at the door. I glanced at Devon, who immediately went to answer it. He didn't even check to see who it was—which instantly told me he knew.

Jake narrowed his eyes as he turned to look in the direction of the door as the entire posse marched in. Matilda first, followed by Prudence, my mom, Hope, Marcy, and...holy cannoli, Rosa. I distinctly remembered the decision was *not* to bring Dani's mom to Luckland. The ladies, however, always did whatever they wanted.

Expecting Dani to be delighted to see her mother, I grimaced when she didn't react other than offering a dim-witted smile.

"Hello, Mother, ladies, good to see everyone," she said as if she saw them all the time. She hadn't seen her mom in at least six months.

His face impassive, Jake remained seated. The women, however, wore their fierce warrior expressions as if they expected to go into battle. I hadn't told Devon why he needed to come home—that I was worried about Dani, but my text would have alerted him, and he'd alerted the ladies, so it wasn't all that surprising they'd come guns blazing. I sat back and decided to let them all do their thing.

I glanced at Dani, hoping she'd at least crack a smile at me. Nothing. Her beautiful and usually expressive eyes were glazed over as if unaware of anything. No. She looked as if she didn't *care* about anything.

Suddenly, a mental image of that asylum in New Mexico surfaced. The people in the photos I'd seen during my research looked stupefied, which was the same expression Dani had. Rosa stared at her daughter, despondent. I headed over to where Rosa stood and gave her a hug and a kiss.

"I'm so glad to see you," I whispered. "Don't worry. Devon will fix everything. I promise you." I had so much faith in Devon that even though I didn't know what was wrong with Dani, I knew he'd sort it out, and Rosa relaxed just a little.

I went back to my seat, glared at Jake, and looked expectantly at Devon. The room was eerily quiet. Jake clenched his knees together, almost as if trying to stop a nervous tic. Good. Let him sweat. Whatever he'd done to Dani, I wanted to see done to him twenty times over.

"So, Jake. Is that short for Jacob?" Devon asked as if we were having a casual conversation.

Jake shrugged. "I suppose it might be."

"The name Burns. Any relation to Arnold? I did some work with him down in Key Biscayne a few years back. That's where you're from, isn't it?"

Jake's leg started to bounce, and he pressed a hand against it while glancing anxiously at the door. "Um, yeah, sure. Arnold is a cousin of mine."

Devon's mouth twitched. I leaned forward, eager to hear more.

"Too bad about that accident. I felt kind of bad, but that's how it goes sometimes," Devon said.

I glanced at him pretty, sure Arnold Burns didn't exist. I supposed that was how detectives worked. They set traps. I was learning something new every day.

"Yes, true, I suppose," said Jake.

"You know that's something we all need to watch out for. There's always that danger. You know, when someone is under the influence," Devon said, continuing with his trap.

"I avoid the stuff myself," said Jake in a somewhat superior tone. "Always need to maintain control, you know."

"Funny you should say that, Jake. It brings me to my next question."

"What's that?" he asked.

"Where did you learn hypnosis?"

I gasped. Dani was hypnotized? I had *not* seen that coming. The women never reacted, and I wondered what Devon had told them before they all got here. Devon must have either guessed or figured out Jake had used hypnosis on Dani, but how did Devon work that out?

Jake didn't answer, but his taut glances from one person to another spoke volumes. The ladies had positioned themselves to block the way to the kitchen, the front door, and the windows.

"Shall I guess then?" asked Devon. "I think your father taught you."

Jake glared at Devon but remained mute.

"What's the release word? You've got all of thirty seconds."

Jake jumped up and beelined it to the door, but before he got more than a couple of feet, Devon grabbed Jake's shirt and tackled him to the ground.

"What's the word, Jake?" Devon growled. When Jake didn't answer, Devon grabbed Jake's arm and twisted it behind his back. Then Devon brought Jake's other arm to join the first and slapped cuffs on him. Pretty darn smooth. I'd never seen Devon in action quite like that before.

"Say it, Jake," Devon commanded. "Say it now, or I'll let the women decide what happens next."

"I get to decide, Devon," said Rosa almost in a whisper. "He tells us now, or *el dormirá en la guarida de un oso esta noche.*"

Oh. Spanish. Not a good sign.

Eyes wide, Jake struggled. "What is she saying?"

"I believe she said you will sleep with the bears tonight," said Marcy, her tone matter-of-fact. Marcy spoke several languages fluently.

"What the hell does that mean?" Jake curled his lip and tried to shake free of Devon's hold.

"It means, my friend, and I use the term loosely, that you'll end up a tasty snack for a grizzly," Devon said, smirking.

An angry Jake was quite an ugly Jake. I had no idea what Dani saw in the creep, but if Devon was right and Jake had hypnotized Dani, it didn't explain why she was perfectly normal the last time I saw her because she was already dating him. That didn't make sense.

Devon gripped Jake's shoulder and squeezed. "One last chance, Jacob," he said. "What's the word to bring her out of it?"

"Pearlanne," he practically screamed. "Okay? It's Pearlanne, you freaking morons!"

I looked at Dani, hoping it would work. She glanced around the room, almost as if trying to figure out what she was doing there. I went straight over and grabbed her hand.

"Dani?"

She shook her head as if to clear it. Rosa quickly strode over and sat down on the other side of Dani before taking her other hand.

"*Mi hija, mi corazón, estás bien. Estás bien.*"

I let go of Dani so Rosa could embrace her. Everyone remained quiet except Jake.

"You gonna let me go now?" he asked. "I gave you the damn word. Take these stupid things off."

"Not a chance, buddy. You're under arrest, and you're coming with me. Let's go." Devon nodded at me, and I nodded back, hoping my expression showed my gratitude.

Devon hauled Jake to his feet, then escorted him out the door. My mother closed the door behind them, and all the ladies gathered about, sitting wherever they could.

Dani looked around again, her eyes a little clearer. "What the hell just happened, and why are we all here like this?"

"Dani, honey, what's the last thing you remember?" her

mother asked.

"Honestly? Jake and I were having dinner. I don't remember much else. I know you had texted me, Pip, and you said you needed me. I think I told Jake I wanted to come home, but that's it."

"That had to be Monday night. That must be when he hypnotized you, Dani. That's why you don't remember anything."

Dani frowned. "No. I think... I think he started way before that. It's still a bit foggy, but I don't even think I liked him at first. Then at some point, I started to feel as if I should give him a chance." She looked up at me. "I told you he was the one, didn't I? Oh god. How could he have done that to me?"

My mom stood. "Dani, you stay here with Pippa. Rosa, why don't you also stay here and catch up with Dani. The rest of us, let's vamoose. Pip, I'll text you later, and we'll put something together for tonight."

Of course they would because all eventful chapters in our lives ended in a Luckland Ladies soiree. That was the gist of it. When one spoke, they spoke for all, and there was no rebuttal. Not that I wasn't okay with the plan, but sometimes it was hard to fathom how they operated in sync like that. The rest of them stood and marched out the door.

I left Dani and her mom to chat, grabbed my laptop and camera, and headed out back. They needed some time alone, and I'd totally neglected my blog. What with kidnapping, aliens, and evil hypnotists, I hadn't had time for blogging.

Just as I got comfortable, my phone buzzed. I shook my head and sighed.

Devon: They've arrested Jonathan.
Me: Where? How? Why?
I didn't know which question to ask first.
Devon: Murder.

CHAPTER THIRTY

DEVON: RED? NOT A WORD. TO ANYONE.

Not telling a secret was the worst thing Devon could have asked me, but after all the recent revelations, I understood why he might not want to tell the ladies that Prudence's ex had murdered someone. When he was ready, I was sure Devon would let them know. In the meantime, my mind swirled with possibilities of who the victim was and if they were someone associated with Prudence—like Wally or Teddy.

Devon had said that Jack had probably learned hypnosis from his father, so did that mean Jonathan had used hypnosis on Wally to get him to disappear? Or on Teddy to get him to run out in front of that garbage truck?

Had Jonathan hypnotized *Pru*? Was that why she believed aliens had landed on Earth?

My brain was just about ready to explode.

As late morning turned into early afternoon, I decided lunch would be a good distraction. Inside, Dani and Rosa nestled comfortably in the family room, holding hands and chatting on the sofa. I often wished I had that kind of relationship with my mom, but I just wasn't as close to her as I was with my dad.

Sometimes I wondered if her filtered connection with Babs and me had anything to do with the fact that Mom tragically lost her parents when she was seventeen.

Rosa looked up and smiled. "Ah, Pippa, I hear you've got quite the thing going with Devon."

I looked at Dani suspiciously. Normally, she'd never gossip about me. Not with her mother. She shook her head and laughed.

"Not me. My lips were sealed. Promise."

I gave Rosa a sidelong glance, daring her not to tell me.

"Your mother told me, sweetie. I think it's wonderful," she said.

"Um, thank you." I supposed it would be wonderful, but I still smarted from my rather embarrassing declaration in the RV. I'd attempted to block that moment from my mind and failed miserably.

As if Dani sensed my discomfort, she stood. "Who's up for pizza? I'll make a food run."

"Why don't we go down to the café? I could do with a walk." In reality, I wanted to get the disturbing thoughts out of my head that Jonathan was a murderer, and his son was a rogue who had tried to take advantage of my best friend.

We ended up in the back corner table at the Blue Sky Café where we ordered a super extra-large pizza. No sooner had we ordered than Devon walked in, looking pretty sharp in his new police chief uniform that must have arrived earlier that day. We had some fun picking one out, though we'd had to search several suppliers because Devon wanted something not too dorky and certainly not military. We ended up ordering a few embroidered polo shirts, some nice black chinos, and a jacket. As he walked in, it was obvious we'd done well. The aquamarine shirt matched his eyes. I picked the color, though I didn't tell him why. It was my little secret—one I would always keep.

His arrival set butterflies loose in my stomach again. Every damn time he showed up unexpectedly, it was the same thing. I wondered if it would always be like that.

He made a beeline for our table, pulled up a chair, and sat down. "Good afternoon, ladies. I have it on good authority we'll be gathering at my mom's tonight, so I thought I'd swing by and tell you all. Five-thirty sharp, she said."

"Might I ask, oh omniscient one, how you knew where to find us?" I asked.

He grinned. "Call it a hunch."

More than likely, he'd used the tracker he'd put on my phone, but if it comforted him to know where I was, then I didn't mind.

"I hope you've got Jake locked up tight," I said for Dani's benefit.

"Don't worry. I transported him to Denver, and he's with the authorities there." He turned to Dani. "When you're ready, I'll get a statement from you, okay?"

Dani nodded, but as her face paled, I changed the subject and pointed to Devon's shirt. "I see your uniform arrived. Any news on your patrol car?"

Devon sat back in his chair. "I've been told it could take a few months. Apparently, there's a backlog of orders to fill before mine, so it looks as if I'll need to keep renting the sedan we picked up at the airport."

I was instantly reminded of our flight back from Flagstaff and the reasons the ladies had abandoned us there. To think they'd kidnapped a murderer and had him tied up in my mom's basement—and Devon had let him go. I was sure he regretted that now.

When the pizza arrived, Devon helped himself to a slice, then said he had to be off. I watched him go, wondering when he was going to tell everyone that Jonathan murdered someone and who it was. Devon knew it was hard for me not to say anything, so he had to let everyone know soon. I hoped.

After we finished the pizza, Rosa smiled. "How about a bit of shopping? Us girls could do with spending some time together doing something we love."

I instantly relaxed. "That's an excellent idea."

"Good. I'll text your mom."

At Dani's startled glance at me, I almost laughed because she knew as well as I did that if one woman texted the other, they all ended up with the same text.

Minutes later, as Dani and I browsed through the new arrivals at Luckland's only clothing boutique, the little bells above the door jingled, and the entire posse showed up.

"Dani, this would be stunning with your coloring," Prudence said as she pulled a dress off the rack.

"Oh, Kate," exclaimed Matilda. "Pip will look smashing in this, don't you think?"

Hope also got involved, finding all sorts of accessories and holding them up against the dresses the ladies had picked.

I looked at Dani, who looked just as curious as I felt. "What do you think they're up to?" she asked in a whisper. "This isn't normal, even for them."

"I assumed they were here to cheer you up, but you're right, they're definitely up to something." I frowned. "Perhaps if we play along, they'll buy us all this stuff." There was something to be said for shopping therapy when you didn't have to pay for it.

We took the dresses they'd chosen for us, and we disappeared into the dressing room. Truthfully, the women had taste. The simple coral sheath Prudence had picked for Dani hugged her body and perfectly complemented her exotic tropical appearance.

I eyed the emerald-green sleeveless dress Matilda had selected. I generally avoided green as I felt it made my skin look pale and my hair appear like a fire hydrant. This dress, however, gave me more of an ethereal mien.

"Wow," said Dani.

"Really?"

"Yep. That's the one."

We went out to model the dresses they'd chosen for us, and the ladies nodded and murmured compliments. Feeling fabulous, I had an idea. After the recent events in Luckland, maybe they all needed a moral boost.

"We need to find something for all of you as well!" That got them all excited. They quickly headed to the racks, sliding items left, right, and back again.

While we had the chance, Dani and I changed back into our street clothes. We returned just as Rosa held up a dress triumphantly.

"Pru, this is the one for you," she said with no room for argument. She sounded just like Dani. Or the other way around.

Prudence appeared hesitant but went with Rosa into the dressing room. A few minutes later, they came back out without showing us a thing, but they were smiling.

"We'll surprise you later," Pru said. "Tillie, your turn."

Not counting the recent disco convention, we hadn't seen Matilda don anything other than a smock dress for quite a long time. Prudence grabbed something from my mom, then grabbed Matilda, almost dragging her to the dressing room. It was another of those moments where I caught a glimpse of the younger versions of themselves. Enlightening. I wished I had my camera to capture the moment. Pru and Matilda were in the dressing room for a while. I swore I heard giggling. The other ladies started to disappear back there as well. Eventually, they all reappeared, carrying their chosen outfits.

Matilda took everything to the front to pay while the others acted pleased with themselves.

Outside, Matilda handed Dani and me our new treasures. "Now, girls, we expect you to arrive promptly tonight, and wear these. I believe we all deserve to look and feel our best."

Though I would have loved to trust that was the only reason for her instruction, I still believed the posse were up to something. By the look on Dani's face, she thought so too.

"Dani," I said. "When this is over, you and I are headed to Cabo. Deal?"

"Not without me, you're not," Devon said right in my ear. I inwardly sighed. Nothing was sacred in Luckland. Nothing.

I turned to face him. "Why are you here, Dev? This is girl territory."

"I'm afraid this is a public sidewalk, my dear, and I am patrolling." He leaned in and kissed me—a public display of affection right there in the middle of Luckland. Dani whistled, and the posse grinned as they waved and walked away. Just then, a car zipped past at a fairly good clip.

"Later," he said, running across the street then hopping into his rented sedan. Reaching out the driver's window, he placed one of those portable flashing lights on the roof of the car and took off after the unfortunate speeder.

Dani, Rosa, and I headed back to my house, where we spent the rest of the day prepping to look our best, and I had to admit, it felt good to get dressed up.

Just before we were ready to leave, I got a buzz on my phone.

Devon: Meet you there. Errand to run.

CHAPTER THIRTY-ONE

D ANI AND I DECIDED TO MAKE A PROPER ENTRANCE, AND TO DO THAT, timing was everything. Devon would be punctual, so us girls made sure to be a few minutes late.

Just as we arrived at Matilda's, Prudence turned up, and I immediately held up my hand. "Do not take another step, Pru. I have to get a picture because you look stunning!" Her jersey dress was a simple navy blue, and she hadn't tossed her hair atop her head in the usual messy bun. Instead, she wore it down. Her thick, wavy, and sexy auburn locks loosely framed her face. She'd also applied soft, dreamy makeup—not her customary bold colors.

I grabbed my camera from my Jeep, then took several pictures of Pru, Dani, and Rosa. I wanted to bring my camera inside to capture what I assumed would be equally stunning women but decided to come back for it later—a camera around my neck was not a good accessory. Rosa and Dani linked arms, as did Pru and I, and we made our way around the back, carefully stepping on the flagstones Devon had laid on the side of the house in case I ever wanted to wear heels.

I doubted there would be many reasons to wear heels, but as this was one of them, I was grateful for his forethought.

We all headed up the steps to the sprawling bi-level back deck and stood at the top. I immediately locked my gaze on Devon's. He stood at the railing, leaning back, drink in one hand.

My previous grand entrances had been pretty amazing, but that one? He didn't move. Didn't smile. Didn't say anything. I waited a heartbeat or two, then smiled—my sexy come-hither smile reserved only for him. It was a very hot moment—until I noticed the man next to him. I must have been too focused on Devon not to notice a stranger. He elbowed Devon, knocking him out of his stupor.

Devon grinned and shook his head. I grinned back, though the heat in my cheeks pretty much screamed my embarrassment. At an audible gasp behind me, I turned to see Deputy Martin looking equally stunned at Pru. It seemed she'd made an impression on him too.

I faced Dani. "Come on, let's get a drink." She nodded, then stopped in her tracks. Following the direction of her gaze, I realized she'd spotted the man next to Devon. He'd also spotted her, and if I thought Dev and I had electricity, theirs was off the charts. Tall and muscular, his skin just a shade darker than Dani's, he had the most extraordinary, chiseled face and was about as attractive as they came. I must have stared too long at him because Devon scowled.

Then Matilda stepped out onto the deck, and oh, my stars, she was a knockout. Gone was the gray hair, replaced by a beautifully stylish cap of ebony. She had dressed in an awesome, sparkly flapper dress, complete with a sparkly band about her forehead. Rather than her outfit making her look as if she were headed to a costume party, she made it seem perfectly in vogue. My mom, Hope, and Marcy were also dressed to kill. Of course,

Babs looked her beautiful self. I definitely had to do a photo shoot.

The posse all gathered at the side of the deck, hugging one another, whispering, and laughing. It was truly joyful and remarkable all at once. I wanted that for Dani and me someday, and I sensed that witnessing moments like these were a gift—something to cherish and tuck away for future reference.

Devon took a few strides over and greeted me properly. While I had the chance, I pulled him to a slightly quiet corner. "Are you going to tell me who Jonathan murdered?"

"All in good time."

"Devon. The suspense is killing me."

"I know, but I wanted—"

"All right, everyone, if I might have your attention," said Matilda. "Let's all have a drink or two, then a bite to eat, then Devon has some news!"

I squeezed Devon's arm. "News? You mean you're going to tell everyone tonight?" I asked, a hopeful tone in my voice.

Devon grinned. "But of course, buttercup. You don't think I'd keep you in suspense, do you?"

"What about your friend?"

"Simon? Well, he's the one who's been helping me, so I thought it only fitting he be here."

Before I could react, Devon motioned Simon to join us.

"Simon, this is Pippa."

"It's nice to meet you, Simon." I instantly remembered during that one night in the infamous Luckland Inn, Devon had quietly spoken to someone named Simon on the phone. This must be him.

"Simon and I worked together for a while," Devon said.

Simon laughed. "We trained together, worked together, spent our off hours together."

He had a wonderful accent. I couldn't quite place it, but it had a musical lilt. French? No, he was clearly American. "Where are you from, Simon?"

"New Orleans."

I smiled. That explained the accent. He glanced over to my right, and I figured Dani must be close by, so I turned and grabbed her arm.

"Simon, this is Dani," I said, trying not to grin. They eyed each other like candy, which, if nothing else, might help her recover from Jake the Jerk. Not that she was heartbroken. Earlier, we'd had a few minutes to talk, and she told me she didn't even remember kissing the guy. I'd crossed my fingers that nothing physical happened between them, or if it had, she never found out.

Matilda clapped her hands and announced dinner was ready. She'd set up a buffet-style table for casual dining that allowed us to serve ourselves, which was unusual for Matilda. She usually organized a more formal affair with name cards. Not that I wanted a sit-down dinner. A buffet was more my style.

Devon, Simon, Dani, and I grabbed the smallest table and took our plates over to the buffet. As soon as I saw the spread, I glanced at Devon, biting back a smile but raising my eyebrows. Cajun. Obviously, Matilda knew Devon had invited Simon, which explained all the gorgeous dresses. The ladies must have wanted Dani to feel just as gorgeous in front of the hot new guy.

Devon laughed. "Easy, Red."

"Easy for you to say, secret agent man. We knew the women were up to something. You could have warned me."

"It was a—"

"Don't you dare!"

He immediately kissed me.

Simon laughed, watching us. "I never thought I'd see the day, Marks," he said before he shook his head.

"What day is that, Simon?" I asked, but I knew what he meant.

He just smiled and turned his attention to Dani. I wanted to eavesdrop, but Devon slowly slid his hand up my thigh, acting like a teenage boy trying to score. I could have slapped his hand away, but I kind of liked it.

After we'd eaten our fill, Devon stood.

"As you are all aware, we've had a relatively eventful few days, well, few weeks. However, I'm happy to say that with the help of Pippa and my good friend Simon here, we've managed to solve several mysteries impacting all of us. Particularly Prudence and Dani.

Dani lifted her chin, refusing to look like a victim, and I leaned over and held her hand, silently praising her for her strength.

"This morning, Simon took Jonathan Steppenhoffer into custody."

Nobody else knew of Jonathan's arrest, so their gasps were quite predictable. They all began chattering, so Devon held up his hand for silence. I sat forward, waiting to hear the name of Jonathan's victim.

"Steppenhoffer has now been charged with Wally Noble's murder."

CHAPTER THIRTY-TWO

I turned to Prudence. Her face was ashen. Thankfully, Martin was next to her, his arm protectively about her shoulders. By his calm expression, he already knew about Jonathan. I glanced back at Devon, who obviously had more to say.

"I'm going to turn this over to Simon for a minute, as I asked him to do the background on Jake Burns, and it was Simon who unraveled this part."

Simon stood up and joined Devon. They were quite the pair and could have been cast in a TV detective show.

"I'm going to start by saying that Jake Burns had a pretty empty search result at first, which for someone who allegedly travels the world doing treasure dives would be unusual. If he were successful, there'd be registered discoveries. Let's just say I didn't like what I wasn't finding." He gave Dani a quick look. "So, I took a little trip down to the Gulf."

I glanced at Dani. She had been diving in the Gulf. That was where she had just flown in from. Alarm bells started ringing.

"Can I ask when you took this trip, Simon?"

"Oh, this was about a month ago."

So, he'd investigated Jake long before anyone asked Devon

to do so. Devon and I knew about Jake, but nobody else had back then. Therefore, Devon started the investigation on his own. Dani and I exchanged meaningful looks. Then I turned my attention back to Simon.

"Long story short, I began to suspect that Jake Burns had a history, and I did some digging. It took a while, I'm sorry to say. We now know that Jake is Jonathan Steppenhoffer's son. Seems Jake did a DNA test a few years ago and found Jonathan. They must have hit it off." Simon shook his head. "Like father like son, I suppose. In any case, the two started a little grifter scheme, roaming the country looking for investors into a treasure-hunting company they formed."

Dani spoke up then. "You mean the clients that were on the dives with us? They were being bilked?"

"Afraid so, and not just the ones you met. Jonathan and Jake also went after silent partners, like widows and venture capitalists, but the duo had certain...methods of persuasion to get people to hand over their money. They also dangled a carrot. Jonathan claimed he knew where Luckland's gold was, that one of the original town founder's descendants told him. From the information Belle told Pippa and Devon, it was Winston McConnell II."

"What does that have to do with Wally?" I asked.

Devon and Simon glanced at each other. "I looked deeper into Jonathan," Simon said. "According to the information you and Devon found, Jonathan already knew of the supposed gold when he met Prudence. When the ladies had Jonathan... restrained, he admitted he wanted to know what Prudence knew about the gold. After I arrested him, he told me he needed to get rid of Wally to get to Prudence, so he turned Wally mad. The same way he later tried to make Prudence believe in aliens."

Pru shook her head. "I don't understand."

"It's a complicated story, but my part was discovering factual evidence. Devon sent me samples of the alien-looking statue that shattered in Colin's workshop, which we tested. The statue was just a composite material, but the luminescent vial buried inside turned out to be Wally."

"How did you know it was Wally?" asked Hope.

"DNA," said Simon. "We located a sweater in an evidence locker in Denver from when he disappeared."

"Oh yes, his favorite cardigan," said Pru. "I gave it to the investigating officer."

"Jonathan killed Wally and took his body to an incinerator. To ensure nobody ever discovered his remains, he went to a glassblower and said they were his grandmother. Jonathan asked the glassblower to create a memento." Simon nodded at Devon, who took over.

"Jonathan hid the vial in the alien-looking statue we affectionally called Elroy."

"The one in my basement," said Pru.

"Well, yes and no. The one you found in the trunk of your car and put in your basement was the one Jonathan bought from the IUAS. He had another one made to look exactly like it. Years ago, he broke into your basement and swapped the two. In his mind, he believed he could pin Wally's death on you. After connecting with Jake, Jonathan changed his mind and decided to permanently get rid of the evidence. Pippa thought the explosion was someone trying to destroy the statue, and she was right." Devon smiled at me. "Jonathan didn't know Prudence had brought it to Colin."

"What about the other one I found out by my car that night? Where'd that one come from?" Prudence's voice was shaky.

"It was the original statue. Jonathan left it there because he's sick in the head. He took delight in frightening you because he knew you still believed aliens had landed on Earth."

"How?"

Devon's gaze turned sympathetic. "Jonathan was adept at hypnosis. A master. He trained Jake, who used it against Dani. Jonathan used it against you."

Martin took Prudence's hand and squeezed it.

"So, you're telling me there are no aliens?" Pru almost sounded disappointed.

"I'm sorry, Pru, but I'm afraid not," said Devon.

"We told you the aliens weren't real, honey," said Matilda, her tone kind.

"What about Teddy? The device?" Prudence asked.

"Teddy was a victim too. The device was nothing more than a toy."

"One more question, if you please, Devon." Prudence glanced around at her friends before setting her shoulders. "If I was hypnotized. Is there a release word?"

Devon took a deep breath. "Yes, but he wouldn't give it to us."

A heated grumble spread throughout the posse, and Prudence's face fell.

Angry at the cruel and diabolical professor, I refused to let Prudence continue to suffer. "It can't be anything any of us have ever said in front of Prudence, but it's not unreasonable to think it came from her and Jonathan's research."

"That's brilliant, Pippa," my mom said with a smile in my direction.

"I have the research pages bookmarked on my phone. Let me pull them up." I quickly opened the browser and called up the articles before leaning closer to Devon so he and Simon could see. They stared at the screen, and Devon scrolled periodically.

Devon looked up. "Extraterrestrial?"

We all stared at Prudence, but she didn't react.

"Alien interactions," Simon uttered.

"Alien reproduction," Devon said.

I shook my head. "I think he'd make it more complicated than that." I took the phone off Devon and went back to one of Pru's research papers. *Human and extraterrestrial sexual interactions and reproductive theory.* In the middle of the paper, there was a subheading. "Sexually Deviant Extraterrestrials," I said, looking right at her.

Prudence tipped her head, then blinked slowly. "They weren't real." Her whispered words sounded loud in the silence. "All this time, they were real to me, yet now they aren't." She regarded her oldest and dearest friends. "You all are the most wonderful friends in the world. I clearly lost my mind, thanks to that son of a bitch, and you stuck with me all these years." Her voice cracked, and tears slid down her face. She stood and held out her arms. The ladies needed no further invitation. They rushed over for a massive group hug, squealing and crying.

Eventually, they broke apart. Prudence settled in Martin's embrace, and Matilda turned to the rest of us, smiling triumphantly.

"Well, it looks as if we've solved the question of the explosion in Pru's basement, the mysterious origins of Elroy, Prudence's misadventures in matrimony, Dani's recent brush with one of the hypnotic duo, and the question of aliens in our midst. I'd say that's quite enough for one evening. Anyone up for karaoke?"

As the ladies discussed who would go first, I pulled Devon aside. "How did you get all that information out of Jonathan?"

"Actually, Jake told us most of it. He wanted a deal. A reduced sentence if he gave us all the goods on his father. Jonathan denied some of it, but when Simon asked him about the hypnosis, Jonathan couldn't help but gloat. He even admitted making Pru forget about the photo of him and Elroy so she wouldn't associate him with the statue. The one thing he wouldn't give us was the release word."

"Well, it doesn't matter now. Prudence no longer believes in little green men. One thing though. I assume the note Pru found on her doorstep was to get her out of the house?"

"Yes. Jake said his father told him he hired someone to destroy the statue, which Jake believed was in Pru's basement because Dani told him."

"That she saw when we did our Halloween trick to get candy." I sighed. It was hard to believe the lengths some people would go to because of greed. "The last few weeks we've heard more about Luckland's gold than we have our whole lives. There *has* to be more to the legend, and I'm positive our meddlesome matriarchs know something."

Devon nodded. "More secrets."

"So, we still need to find the boxes, research the original founder's map, and perhaps dig deeper into our history and family tree." I'd thought I hadn't needed to find more about the founders and their descendants, but I had a hunch there were more hidden treasures in that line of investigation. That was a lot of work, but I felt it needed to be done. Nothing was as it seemed in Luckland.

"Devon, my boy." Matilda sidled up to her son. "You're up."

Up?

Devon grinned and took the mic from her. I stared open-mouthed. Devon never did karaoke. He wrapped an arm around my waist, and as the smooth intro began, tears filled my eyes.

Then he started singing the Barry White ballad, *You're My First, My Last, My Everything*. Right then, I knew Devon was making a declaration and responding to my embarrassing announcement on the RV. He was doing the one thing in the world that could make me his forever.

When the song ended, I stood on my toes, pulled his face down to mine, and kissed him with everything I had. Ignoring the whistles and rounds of applause, I indicated Devon pass the mic to Tillie, who grinned like a fool, then I took Devon by the hand and led him around to the side of the house.

He leaned up against the wall and put his hands around my waist. I placed mine around his neck, and as the sun dipped beyond the horizon and a blaze of pink painted the sky, we stood and smiled at each other.

"Say, Red." His low voice held a slight rasp. Incredibly sexy. "You know we're meant to be, you and I."

I studied his face, memorizing every detail, like the faintly emerging crow's feet, the singular dimple on his right cheek, and those beautiful long dark lashes. It was a face I'd known my whole life, but until that exact moment, I'd never quite fully seen.

"Perhaps we always have been." My throat was so tight I could barely breathe.

Maybe we didn't actually say those three words, but we didn't need to.

A few weeks later, out on my back porch and under the spectacular midnight blue Colorado sky that twinkled with stars, we were having another perfect moment cuddled under a blanket with a bottle of wine.

Babs: Pippa! Emergency! Get over to the money pit, now!

SNEAK PEEK AT THE NEXT LUCKLAND MYSTERY
MISLAID LOVE AND FOUND BODIES

CHAPTER ONE

Babs: Pippa! Emergency! Get over to the money pit, now!

I stared at the text and groaned. Not just because my twin sister had ruined my perfect moment with Devon and me under the spectacular midnight blue Colorado sky that twinkled with stars, but because the money pit she referred to was my future home. The house was part of an old estate purchased as a gift by my mother and her BFFs—Luckland's finest crew of rabble-rousers.

"What is it?" Devon asked. He cocked his head and squinted. With a lock of his thick, wavy hair dangling in front of one eye, the man was incredibly adorable.

"Babs. She says there's an emergency at our very own Mystic Manor." I sighed as I texted back a reply, though I doubted it was a real emergency, especially because, as chief of police, Devon would have received a text of his own.

"Well, Red, I guess we'd better be off then," he said.

I used to reflexively kick back at Devon calling me Red, which referred to my mop of red curls, though his nickname was growing on me.

"But first..." He leaned over and kissed me. Long and slow. A kiss I felt all the way down to my toes.

"Well done, Casanova, but we'll never get anywhere if you keep that up," I said when I caught my breath. Laughing, he stood, grabbed my hand, and pulled me up.

Luckland wasn't a large town, so it didn't take long for us to reach the Manor. Babs's car, as well as a few SUVs, stood out front.

We pulled up, got out, and headed to the entrance of our old gothic stone structure, which was under renovation. The door stood wide open.

"Should we go in?" I whispered as I held Devon's hand.

"No time like the present," he whispered back, giving my hand a reassuring squeeze.

We stepped inside the large foyer and, following a cacophony of voices, immediately headed up the frayed, red-carpeted stairs.

The master bedroom suite was in total disarray. Since that particular room required some major updates, we had decided to begin the reno there, and the construction crew had pretty much ripped it down to the studs. Moonlight streamed through the windows, shining a silvery beam on the Luckland Ladies.

I had several names for the ladies, none less descriptive of the mayhem they caused wherever they went, but they consisted of my mom, Kate, along with Devon's mom, Matilda, and the remaining members of their tight-knit posse, Prudence, Hope, and her fiancée Marcy, who all talked at once.

Babs and her husband, Tom, who happened to be the architect in charge of this project, stood quietly by, but Leah, my three-year-old niece, sat upon Tom's shoulders with a bicycle helmet on her head, singing some gibberish that resembled one of her cartoon favorites.

Devon straightened his shoulders and held up his hand for

silence, which basically had no effect. It very rarely had before, so I wasn't surprised it didn't now. He turned to me, his new investigator-in-training since the start of some recent odd mysteries, and nodded. I gave one of my ear-piercing whistles. It did the trick every time.

"Babs, care to tell us what's happening?" Devon asked in the ensuing silence.

"Not a clue. We just got here. Something about strange noises though." She shrugged, helpful, as always. She might be my twin, but we were as fraternal as fraternal twins could be. She was little miss perfect. I was the firecracker.

"I see," said Devon. "Well then, Mom, care to explain?"

"The house needs to be cleansed," she announced, her tone unequivocal.

"It's under construction. Cleaning the house is not an emergency." He looked bewildered. Matilda had that effect on people. She was eccentric and full of surprises. I couldn't anticipate what she'd say or do next. Ever.

"Not cleaned, dear boy, *cleansed!*" she replied as if her explanation was perfectly sensible.

"I think she's talking about smudging again, Dev," I said. Matilda had begun to explore her intuitive side—with a little help from ghost-hunting cable channels.

"Quite right, Pippa," said Prudence. "Tillie has been sensing some very strange goings on, and after the basement incident, we thought it important to investigate."

That was when I began to see some light. One of Prudence's exes had recently tried to blow up her basement, which put the ladies on high alert. I gave Devon a sidelong glance—my hint that he should remain quiet because I was sure more information would follow.

"It *is* October, exactly the time of year to expect oddities," Hope said. Hope was an aspiring playwright, an avid reader, and a former librarian. "Not surprising at all that we heard what we heard."

Devon shook his head, but before he had a chance to say something, my mom spoke up.

"The emergency, Devon, is that something is making a horrifying noise when clearly there should be total silence in here."

Now we were getting somewhere.

"What kind of noise, Mom?" I asked. "I don't hear anything odd. Seems pretty quiet."

My mom held up her hand and looked about. "Shhh. Everyone be quiet for a moment. Listen."

Everyone held their breath, eyes wide as if that allowed them to hear better, and waited. Nothing.

"I'm afraid I don't hear anything," said Devon, using his authoritarian voice, which had about as much effect as holding up his hand.

"Keep listening, my boy," said Matilda. "I promise you'll hear it."

Devon sighed and glanced at me, but he acquiesced. We all repeated the wide-eyed breath-holding ritual—except Leah, who decided to start singing again. Tom took that as his opportunity to make a speedy exit. Coward that he was. Maybe that was harsh, but I was just a wee bit jealous he was allowed to jump ship.

I waited with bated breath, expecting some sort of clanking like old pipes or something, but what broke the silence sounded as if someone had stepped on a cat's tail. Not that I'd ever done so, but I'd seen plenty of viral videos. Maybe there was a feral feline in the attic. I figured I'd let them all speak their mind before I mentioned my sensible and plausible suggestion.

The high priestesses of small-town living stood almost in a huddle and held one another's hands, all looking quite determined as if they were on trial. Melodramatic, as always—right down to their attire. Because it was close to Halloween, I shouldn't have been surprised they were costumed up, but they'd all dressed alike in black leggings and black long-sleeve tops, which did surprise me. If they'd been strangers, they might have been mistaken for cat burglars.

Matilda stepped forward, clearly taking the lead. She stood tall and proud—her usual stance when caught in an awkward situation. She was quite striking, with her cap of ebony hair and fiery blue eyes.

"I assume you two heard that?" She looked from Devon to me and back again. "That is not normal, as I'm sure you'd agree. It's an omen." She glanced at her comrades, who all nodded.

"An omen. I see," said Devon, nodding as if agreeing. "May I inquire as to what you think this is an omen of?"

The women all began chattering at once, offering up a bizarre round-robin of answers, which prompted Devon to hold up one hand in an effort to silence them, then two hands. Finally, he snapped.

"For god's sake, ladies, one at a time!"

That certainly had an impact. I smiled at him, proud he was finally getting the hang of keeping order among the posse.

Babs cleared her throat. "I'm going out on a limb here, but that, most definitely, was a cat. I know that sound."

I blinked. Babs coming forward and saying something while in the middle of the chattering ladies was a rarity, but when she did involve herself, she was most definitely the calm in the center of a Luckland storm. Not because she had some sort of inner serenity—she just wasn't interested in being a problem solver. She focused on herself, her family, and her daily routine. That was about it. So, what made her announcement even more astonishing was that she'd thought what I'd thought. I guess that boded well for me.

"Leah often, accidentally, of course, trips over Fester. That is the sound he makes," she said.

I nodded. "I thought the same thing, though not from first-hand experience."

Babs sidled over to stand next to me, which was an act of bonding and our wall of defense because we knew what we were about to encounter.

"Girls, that is not a cat," said our mother, her expression haughty. "Not even close."

"How about we all reconvene this discussion outside," said Devon. It seemed he'd had enough and wanted the women out of the house.

I'd taken a step to head down the stairs when the floors and walls suddenly shook, and something, be it cat or evil creature from hell, went careening through the air and out the bedroom window, shattering the glass.

CHAPTER TWO

THE NEXT FEW MINUTES WERE LIKE A SCENE FROM A TEEN HORROR movie. Instead of the teen screamers, however, the group running out the door was a horde of sixty-year-olds, followed by three thirty-year-olds, one of whom, I was sure, wished he'd stayed at home. In any case, we all ended up out front.

"What was that?" I asked no one in particular.

Devon turned to me. "I'll go and check. You and everyone else stay here."

I wasn't going anywhere, but I was curious to know what my mother and her band of friends were doing at my house in the first place.

I grabbed my sister's arm and directed her to the curb, where I pulled her down to sit next to me. The women stood smack dab in the middle of the front yard, all talking at once, their tone hushed so we couldn't hear a word.

I turned to Babs. "Okay, want to tell me what everyone was doing in the house?"

"Honestly, Pip, I have no idea. Mom texted me to come over, so I did. I don't know what they were up to."

I didn't think the women knew what they were up to half

the time, but there was always something going on with them. Figuring out what that might be was the challenge.

"All right, I'm going to go ask. See what I can find out."

I stood, brushed off the dust on my jeans, then headed over to the women. "Mom?"

"Yes, Pip, what is it?" She acted as if standing in the middle of my yard after running out of my house because something creepy happened in there was a perfectly normal situation, which, considering what we'd all gone through the last few months, probably was.

"Why are you all here?" I asked.

"Because we were attacked by a flying creature, Pippa. Why else?"

"No. Mom. What were you all doing in my house?" I'd learned early on that the first rule with the Luckland Ladies was to be direct.

"What do you mean?" she asked. "Where should we have been?"

"I don't know. Your house? Tillie's? Pru's? Anywhere but *my* house."

"Technically, dear, it's not quite yours yet."

"Well, that's a low blow, Mom. Are you taking back your gift?"

"Don't be silly. I don't know what's gotten into you. We came over because we were planning a sur..."

"Don't say it, do not say that word." If there was one thing in this world I detested, loathed, and was unable to cope with, it was a surprise. Nobody was allowed to surprise me. Nobody —unless it was so fabulous, I made an exception. Like when Devon bought me an antique locket at a yard sale. That was an acceptable surprise. Otherwise, surprises were a phobia of mine. I liked to know exactly what was happening. Probably because growing up in Luckland, there was a never-ending supply of surprises. Nothing was ever as it seemed.

"We had a lovely idea for the master suite, and we just wanted to take a look at the progress and figure out a few things, that's all," she said. "Neither here nor there at this point. It seems there are bigger issues at play."

"The flying creature?"

"Of course. We must find out what it was."

"*We* don't need to do anything. Let Devon handle it."

After a non-verbal conversation with her friends, where they just looked at one another, my mom nodded. "Fine, we'll go. Did you want a ride, or will you wait for Devon?"

"I'll wait, of course." I wasn't really keen on waiting in the dark while he searched the yard for some poor dead critter, but it beat the alternative. After everyone had gone, including Babs, I sat back down on the curb, then quickly stood again, trying not to imagine what might be scurrying around the yard, or worse, and wishing I'd taken that ride.

"Boo!"

I think I jumped six feet in the air.

"That was so not funny," I said once my heart stopped racing.

Devon grinned. "I couldn't resist."

Some things would never change. Tormenting me was one of them. Devon was not a particular favorite of mine growing up. He was annoying, a complete nerd, and my chief persecutor, constantly tugging on my pigtails and leaving little creatures in my lunch bag. Then, a few months ago, he'd returned to Luckland, all grown up. *My* grown-up self soon recognized that all the friction between us had miraculously transformed into something far more electric. We were still working out the kinks though.

He grabbed me around the waist and drew me in for a kiss, quickly erasing all memories of mischief.

"Did you find the catapulting creature?" I asked once I'd gotten my breath back.

"No. I think we'll have Tom send some of the crew to look around tomorrow and see if there's some sort of nest in the walls or something."

I considered that for a moment. The idea creatures might have a nest in the walls of my future home did not sit well. "Perhaps it would make more sense to call an exterminator."

"Clearly, Red, the crew ought to be able to find any unwanted creatures."

"Clearly, that's ridiculous, Mighty Mouse. They're carpenters and construction experts, not rodent control."

"Nevertheless, I've already called Tom."

"Then this is an after-the-fact argument?" I was a little peeved at that.

"Of course. But that means we get to have an after-the-completely-unnecessary-argument make up session, right?" His eyes glinted with mischief. I should have huffed off in righteous indignation, but I didn't. I was only human. Instead, I sighed and allowed him to pick me up and carry me off to the car. It was totally worth it.

<hr>

We arrived back at the Manor the following morning, greeted by a crew of workers scurrying about the front lawn—or what would someday be a lawn, planting little stakes with orange flags everywhere. Tom stood on the concrete and stone porch, apparently directing the tradesmen.

We weren't even close to doing any sewer or pipe work yet,

so I had no idea what they were up to. We headed over to where Tom now conferred with a helmeted crewmember.

"Tom, what's all this?" asked Devon.

Tom's expression showed a little consternation as if he hadn't expected us to be there. "Ah, well. We're digging up the yard."

I took another look at the crew, who had all stopped what they were doing and were listening to our conversation.

Devon frowned. "I asked you to find a den of critters in the walls of the house. I didn't ask you to start digging around our yard."

"That's true, Devon, and I apologize, but your mom kind of did." Tom then looked at me. "So did yours, along with the others, and since their names are still on the actual deed to this property, you'll have to take it up with them." He nodded toward the road.

I turned just as the ladies came barreling down the road in my mom's SUV. I squeezed Devon's hand. A silent reminder to put on his diplomatic hat.

"Ladies," he said as they approached, his tone pleasant. "Good morning to you all."

Well done.

"Now, Devon, we can explain." Matilda, knowing him best, probably saw right through his façade.

"Please, Mother, do explain," he replied, his tone now laced with humor, which was a good sign his anger had abated.

She waited for a moment, looking to make sure her partners in crime were by her side. "We were on our way home last night when we suddenly realized what had happened. My intuition was on high alert."

"Yes! As soon as Tillie said she knew, we all knew," exclaimed my mom while nodding emphatically.

"You have a ghost," Hope said.

"A ghost?" I shook my head before I glanced at Devon. He took a deep breath.

"Fine, we have a ghost. That doesn't mean you have to dig up our yard."

"Oh, well, it's the bones, you see. We have to find them."

Devon straightened his spine. "Human bones?"

"No, of course not. Don't be silly, Devon. It's obviously a cat or some other critter."

"So why do you have to find the bones?"

"We have to move them," Prudence declared. "The critter will continue to haunt you otherwise."

"So, you're digging up the yard to get rid of the ghost?" I asked. That was all utter bullshit. The ladies were up to something. Something elusive.

Devon must have also come to the same realization because he gazed at the posse, eyebrow raised. "We appreciate your concern. However, we don't want you digging up *our* front yard."

"Oh, well. Of course, it's your yard," my mother said. "But if we don't find the bones..."

"Leave them where they are," Devon said, voice firm. He turned to me, and it seemed the right time to make an exit.

As we headed toward the car, Devon grabbed my hand. "Is it me, or are they acting weirder than normal?"

"Weirder. Definitely weirder."

"Right. We need to keep a closer eye on them. Are you up for more investigative work, Red?"

I groaned because keeping an eye on the ladies usually spelled disaster.

www.scarsdalepublishing.com

THE LUCKLAND MYSTERY SERIES

Grande Dames and a Vegas Heist
Aliens and the Dearly Departed
Mislaid Love and Found Bodies
Stolen Recipes and a Dead Chef
Vengeful Spirits and a Lost Gold Mine

More to come!